A.T

When Lalia Da... ...edged
Victorian beauty... ...Alvin a
week before he... ...ghted.
Perhaps she dese... ...has been
too proud? To save face she accepts the proposal of
Alvin's cousin, Jerome Brookford—her money in exchange for the security of marriage, even though it will be
a marriage in name only.

Lalia is convinced that she wants nothing to do with
love, but when she discovers her mistake it is almost too
late. For Jerome has gone to his estate in Jamaica and
news has come of a devastating hurricane . . . Can she
reach her husband in time to tell him that he is the man she
really wants?

By the same author in Masquerade:

RUNAWAY MAID
THE DEVIL'S ANGEL

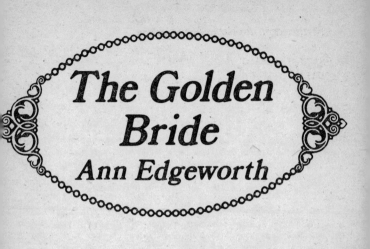

The Golden Bride

Ann Edgeworth

MILLS & BOON LIMITED
London . Sydney . Toronto

First published in Great Britain 1982
By Mills & Boon Limited, 15–16 Brook's Mews,
London W1A 1DR

ISBN 0 263 73804 3

Set in 10 on 11pt Times Roman

Photoset by Rowland Phototypesetting Ltd
Bury St Edmunds, Suffolk
Made and printed in Great Britain by
Cox & Wyman Ltd, Reading

CHAPTER
ONE

'I CANNOT understand why Papa has been so long silent,'
Lalia Darrencourt said restlessly as she turned from the
window where she had been watching the long tree-lined
avenue. 'It is now over two months since we have had a
letter from him.'

Her aunt, Miss Flora, looked up from the cushion cover
in Berlin work on which she was engaged.

'It was in February we heard from him, was it not my
dear?'

'Yes, and now it is April. I know he said then he would
be returning in the first week in April,' Lalia's slender
brows drew together in a worried frown, 'but I find it
strange he has not confirmed it and let us know the exact
date of his return from Spain. For all we know, he may
have changed his mind about returning this month.'

'Oh no, my dear, your Papa was perfectly definite
about returning as soon as his health was restored. He
knows there is much to be seen to before your marriage to
Alvin. Tell me, my love, is this yellow wool too harsh a
shade against the pink rose?'

Lalia crossed the room and stood behind her aunt's
chair to regard the somewhat colourful bouquet of
embroidered flowers.

'It *is* a trifle vivid, Aunt Flora. But if you put some green
between the two colours—a leaf perhaps—I think it will
appear better.'

She wandered back to the window and stood fingering
the heavy fringe of the curtain, her slim figure and fair,

curly hair outlined against the bright spring sunlight. 'It is so unlike Papa to arrive unannounced.'

'Perhaps his letter has been lost,' Miss Flora suggested. 'I do not trust foreign posts. Pray do not distress yourself, dearest child, I feel certain your Papa will arrive any day soon and I have given Mrs Grant orders to prepare his rooms and air his bed.' She raised her head. 'Do I hear riders, my dear?'

Lalia pushed aside the curtains and exclaimed: 'It is Alvin, and he has someone with him.'

'Ah, now your anxieties will all fly away,' Miss Flora said with a sentimental sigh. 'Dear Alvin, such a truly *faithful* lover. You know, your being children together, and your estates adjoining and your love for each other is like a fairy tale. The alliance is the dearest wish of your Papa and Mrs Prior.'

The door opened and the butler announced: 'Mr Prior and Mr Brookford.'

Lalia went to meet them, smiling. 'I'm glad you have come, Alvin. I have been worrying myself because we have not heard for so long from my father, it is so unlike him.'

'Oh, Sir Ashley is probably enjoying the Spanish sun and is not inclined to write letters,' Alvin declared, bestowing a kiss upon her flushed face. 'Miss Flora, I have brought my cousin, Jerome Brookford, to call upon you. Lalia, you must remember Romey, he used to stay with us at Kingsweir when we were children.'

Lalia turned her head to look at the man standing silently behind her fiancé. He was not as tall as Alvin and had none of his startling good looks and easy charm. She saw a thickset young man with dark hair and eyes as blue as her own set under strong dark brows, eyes that were surveying her without the admiration to which she, Miss Lalia Darrencourt, heiress to her father's fortune and declared beauty at her recent presentation to Queen

Victoria, expected and considered as her right.

'Of course I remember him,' she said, offering her hand. 'He once pulled me out of the fish pond at Kingsweir.'

'Where you were trying to catch the goldfish after having been forbidden to go near them.' He took her hand in a firm grasp. 'I trust you are more amenable to authority now.'

Alvin laughed gaily. 'Oh no, not at all, my dear Romey. She is thoroughly spoiled! Her Papa, Miss Flora, the servants and I all obey her slightest commands.'

'Then you are doing her a great injury,' Romey Brookford remarked calmly. 'Nothing warps a nature more certainly than having everything one wants.'

Lalia felt herself stiffen. 'I do *not* have all I want! Oh, you were always a horrid tease!'

'But you have forgiven him,' Alvin chuckled, drawing her to him. 'Romey is to stay with us for a time, he has brought his mother to try the treatment at Harrogate for her rheumatic condition.'

'I am sorry to know she suffers,' Lalia murmured, then turned to Alvin. 'I have just had samples of the wedding invitations and I am not pleased with them so I shall order another design. And I am making plans to visit London shortly for some shopping.'

'What a business it is, this marrying,' Alvin declared in mock dismay, 'Lalia positively neglects me to dream of gowns and shawls and bonnets.'

'Oh, but there is so much to attend to,' Miss Flora said eagerly. 'There is the wedding dress, *such* a charming design in paper-white French brocade—'

'Pray spare him the details, Aunt! He will observe the gown's full glory in the church.'

'I shall be so desperately nervous I know I shall notice nothing,' Alvin assured her.

Lalia was about to speak when a footman entered

carrying a silver salver which he proffered to Miss Flora who drew back, exclaiming in some distress.

'Oh dear! A telegram! It will be bad news, I know it! I cannot open it! Lalia my dear, pray read it to me.'

Lalia picked up the telegram and having read it, cried happily, 'It is from Papa! He sends it from Dover and says we are to send the carriage to Brackton tomorrow to meet the train. How relieved I am!'

'I gather he is fully recovered in health,' Alvin remarked, 'thanks to the doctor's advice to spend a winter in Spain. Lalia, can you ride with us this morning? Romey is never happy unless he has a horse between his knees, and it is a fine day for riding.'

'Yes, of course, but first you must have some refreshment. Aunt Flora will see to it while I change into my riding habit.' She smiled at him and, gathering up the train of her morning gown, hurried from the room.

When she returned, her horse, Betsy, a spirited little bay mare, was being walked to and fro by a groom before the steps of the great house that had been the home of the Darrencourt family for four generations. Winterbridge Hall was one of the largest estates in Yorkshire. Adjoining it lay Kingsweir, home of the Prior family. The two families had long enjoyed friendship and it had been understood, since they were born, that Lalia and Alvin Prior would make a match of it and unite the two estates when Sir Ashley, Lalia's widowed father, should die. Lalia, beautiful, admired, spoiled by her gentle, studious father and soft-hearted aunt, found Alvin a charming lover and companion with whom it was the most natural thing to fall in love and marry. Although she would not admit it, the fact that there were many sore female hearts when the engagement was announced, and the knowledge that she was envied by other girls, was not unpleasing to her. She was beautiful, rich, and was to marry the most attractive man in the county. Naturally she was envied by less fortunate girls.

She set off, riding between her two escorts down the long drive that wound through a fine stand of beeches and into parkland reaching down to the river. They struck across the park and were about to cross the bridge when a groom galloped up with a message for Alvin who frowned and said impatiently,

'My mother demands I return at once! Lady Grange and her daughters have called and I am to make polite conversation with them.' He glanced ruefully at Lalia. 'They are *your* relations, Lalia, so why must they inflict themselves upon us?'

'I am very glad indeed they *have* called on you and not on us,' she said, tilting her head to smile mischievously at him. 'They bore me most distressingly, I assure you. Do you have to go?'

Alvin groaned. 'I'll have little peace with my mother if I don't. Will you come with me?'

'But I haven't had a gallop,' Lalia protested. 'Betsy is pulling my arms out.'

'Then have your gallop with Romey and follow me,' Alvin said, 'and release me from making small-talk with those two simpering little geese.' He raised his crop in salute and rode off.

'Come, let us ride through the fields,' Lalia cried. The cool April air against her face brought her a feeling of delicious excitement. How good life was! A handsome lover, a beautiful home, and her father returning tomorrow recovered in health, and preparations for her wedding in May going smoothly ahead. How stupid people were to say life had shadows. Her life had always been sunshine. She did not miss the mother she had never known, and her father, a studious man whose interest lay in books, had never opposed her wishes and had given her a free hand in everything and although she was only nineteen it was she, rather than Miss Flora, who managed the house and its staff of servants.

'You ride well.'

She turned to the man whose presence she had forgotten in the exhilaration of her gallop. He wore no hat and his thick dark hair tumbled about his forehead. He rode well, she noticed, better than Alvin even. As she met his cool, critical gaze she felt again the faint quickening of irritation inside her.

'Sorry you've had to put up with me,' he said unexpectedly. 'Shall we start back for Kingsweir and relieve Alvin of some of his social duties?'

'I suppose we must,' she sighed, and turned Betsy, who had hoped for another gallop, in the direction of the road. 'Although I have no wish to meet my Aunt Mildred and her two excessively uninteresting girls.'

'But it will be better than having to converse with me.'

She flicked her horse with her whip. 'Why are you so certain I dislike you?'

'Because you do. We quarrelled as children when we met, usually because I would not let you have your own way.'

'I suppose you demanded *your* way,' she flashed at him.

'Most probably,' he agreed. 'You were an extremely pretty little girl and you knew it and counted upon it.'

'But it did not count with you?'

'I didn't let it.' He grinned and the severity of his face lightened for a moment. 'I had other things to think about beside pretty, spoilt little girls.'

'I remember Alvin once said something about your father . . .' she stopped, remembering what it was that Alvin had told her.

'My father was a compulsive gambler,' he spoke with a grimness that momentarily shocked her. 'My childhood was haunted by the results of his craving. It ruined my mother's health, and I was glad when he died.'

Lalia was silent, struck by the bitterness of his words. Alvin had told her how Romey's father had dissipated a large fortune and died leaving heavy debts and an estate drained of money. No wonder his son had no love for him. Something she sensed in Romey, a strong nature held in check, a lack of lighter grace and bleakness of spirit, could be explained by a shadowed life.

But thinking of it made her uncomfortable, it seemed out of tune with her April mood. She gathered up her reins and together they rode on to Kingsweir.

A butler ushered them into the drawing-room where Mrs Prior, Alvin and their guests were sitting.

'Well Lalia, how are you?' Lady Grange's eyes roved over her niece's beautifully-cut riding habit and silk hat with its wisp of veiling. 'Dear me, what a high colour you have, postively bucolic! Your mother had the same high colour and I used to advise her to drink vinegar. My girls are longing to hear of your wedding plans. I suppose you are busy considering bridesmaids?'

Her eyes went to the two girls sitting beside Alvin and it was obvious what was in her mind.

'I have already chosen,' Lalia said carelessly. She had no liking for her aunt or cousins and had never bothered to hide it. 'I have chosen three cousins on my father's side and a London friend.'

Nina, the elder girl, swung around, dismay spreading over her face.

'You mean, you *aren't* going to ask us to . . .' she stopped abruptly, a flush colouring her face pink.

'I suppose we aren't considered grand enough for you!' Harriet, her sister, said furiously.

Lalia shrugged and turned away, well aware of the girls' jealousy. Neither of the Grange girls was likely to marry, they were somewhat plain and ill-educated and without fortune. Their jealousy might have been less if they had been welcome at Winterbridge Hall and asked to some of the social activities there, but Lalia conveniently forgot them when invitations were sent out.

Under cover of conversation, Alvin asked: 'Well, how did you get on with cousin Romey?'

'I feel a little sorry for him,' she said, 'his life has not been a happy one. But he is far too grim and severe in manner. Does he ever laugh?'

'The poor devil hasn't much to laugh at, he's burdened with debts, and the estate is in a bad way, nothing has been done to improve it for years. Even the house, Hildon Manor, is in bad repair.'

'It is in Dorset, isn't it?'

'Yes, not very far from the coast. A fine position and once a fine estate. He'll be forced to sell, I'm afraid. His mother is very delicate, which is an extra burden on him. And he is the only child.'

Shortly before she left, Lalia sought Romey and held out her hand.

'Goodbye Mr Brookford . . . Romey. Thank you for escorting me this morning. I am sorry we do not like each other much, I am most at fault because you *did* pull me out of the fish-pond.'

He looked at her for a moment before speaking and she had the same uncomfortable sensation of being weighed up, with uncomplimentary results.

Then he bowed and said: 'Goodbye Lalia. I wish you and Alvin every happiness in your marriage.'

She murmured her thanks and escaped from the room with Alvin.

He rode with her to Winterbridge Hall, promising to call in a few days to greet Sir Ashley.

She found her aunt deep in planning a meal to celebrate Sir Ashley's return the next day.

'A saddle of mutton, perhaps,' Miss Flora murmured, consulting a small writing tablet. 'Mrs Grant thinks a roast duck to follow . . . and something light for a pudding, Ashley will be tired from his journey and his digestion has always been delicate.'

Lalia agreed absently. Her mind was on the morrow when her father would be home again, his health restored. Then everything would be perfect. They would sit and chat cosily and he would tell her about Spain and she would reveal her plan to visit London for a week to buy wedding clothes. He was always ready to listen and she knew her gay chatter amused him.

When Nancy, her maid, called her next morning, Lalia sprang from bed to peer out of the window. A glorious spring day met her eyes. Pearly mists were retreating before the bright rays of the sun, dew sparkled on every branch and blade of grass and on the lacy cobwebs draping the shrubbery. Tiny clouds floated dreamily in a clear sky and a golden glory of daffodils was spread under the newly-green birches at the end of the lawn. This was a day to welcome her father back to his ancestral home, she thought joyfully. He would be weary, since he had chosen to return via Paris, a city he loved, and the long journey would have taken toll of his energies.

Nancy remarked, as she carefully coiled the bright, silky hair high on her young mistress's head, 'Master'll be right glad to be home again. Foreign places isn't like home, is they, Miss Lalia?'

'Perhaps not, but Spain has given him back his health, thank God,' Lalia said, smoothing back the lace cuffs of her navy poplin dress.

She spent a busy morning arranging flowers the gardener had sent in from the glass-houses, singing happily as she worked. Her aunt fussed around the house, getting in everyone's way and changing her mind every ten minutes on what she wanted done.

At lunch both Lalia and her aunt were too excited to eat much and had their coffee served while sitting in the window of the library from where they could watch the long slope of the avenue.

'Oh dear! How I hate this waiting!' Lalia exclaimed impatiently.

'Ah, my dear, you always did want things to happen when *you* wanted them to,' her aunt told her. 'I used to fear for you—'

But Lalia had ceased to listen; her quick ear had caught the sound of wheels and she jumped up to see the carriage coming up the avenue.

She cried: 'He is come at last!' and ran out through the hall to the front door with her aunt following more sedately. She was at the top of the steps when the footman opened the carriage door and helped her father to alight.

'Papa! Oh how good it is to see you again! How did you . . .' She stopped abruptly, hardly believing her eyes as she saw the small female figure wrapped in shawls follow her father out of the carriage. She heard her aunt's gasp of surprise behind her and watched her father turn and offer his arm to the dark-eyed, voluptuously beautiful young woman before escorting her up the steps.

'Flora, Lalia, my dears,' he smiled gently upon their stunned faces, 'Let me present Rosa who is longing to meet you and whom I know you will welcome into your hearts.'

'Rosa?' Lalia stammered.

'Rosa, my dear wife,' Sir Ashley said proudly. 'We were married a week ago!'

CHAPTER
TWO

FOR a moment Lalia was too stunned to move or speak. She could not have heard aright! Her father's words . . . she had imagined them or had misunderstood. *Married* to this tiny, vivid creature whose great dark eyes were surveying her with a mixture of curiosity and wariness!

Aunt Flora was the first to speak. She moved forward, her plump face pale and the hand she offered trembling slightly.

'I—I bid you welcome. Ashley,' she turned piteously to her brother, 'Why did you not tell us to expect . . . we had no notion you were considering . . .'

Sir Ashley looked from her to Lalia. 'But I mentioned meeting Mrs Carew and her daughters when I first arrived in Cartagena.'

'Yes, you did,' Lalia said breathlessly, 'but you never said you planned . . .'

'My dear, I wrote at great length to tell you how my dear Rosa had made me happy by consenting to be my wife. Surely you received my letter?'

'No, we have received nothing from you since February,' Lalia became aware of the staring servants. 'Oh, do pray come in. I am forgetting . . . It is such a surprise.'

She turned and led the way into the library where a bright log fire blazed in the marble fireplace and sun came mistily through the double curtains looped over the windows.

When she turned to face her father she was in command of herself again although her heart was beating unevenly and she still felt shocked and bewildered. What could have persuaded her father to fall victim to a beautiful girl less than half his age? If only his letter had come and prepared her for this catastrophe! Through tight lips she managed to say, 'I shall order tea, I expect your—wife is tired from the journey.'

'You may call me Rosa,' the girl threw off her shawls and advanced to the fire. 'Oh, how cold England is! I had forgotten. My father was English and I was educated here, you know. I did not like the English school, so many rules and punishments!' She flung back her head, laughing gaily. 'I was a rebel! My mother is Spanish and I am not like the silly meek English girls!'

'I—see. Would you like to go to your room? I will tell Mrs Grant to prepare it for you.'

'Oh no, I shall sit here and get warm; and I do not want tea, I will have coffee.'

'Certainly, my dear,' Sir Ashley said fondly, 'Lalia will see to it. Then you must rest, you have not yet recovered from the steamer.'

Rosa shuddered. 'Oh! Such a dreadful experience! If you had not been with me I should have died of fright!' She smiled up at Sir Ashley.

Lalia turned abruptly. 'I shall order the coffee.'

Her aunt followed her out of the room. They stood in the hall, looking at each other. At last Lalia burst out,

'He is mad! To marry a girl so young—and half Spanish! What made him do it, Aunt Flora? Do you realise she is his *wife*, my step-mother? Oh, it is outrageous, impossible, disgraceful!' She put her hands over her eyes, shivering as a deadly chill crept over her.

Her aunt slipped an arm around her shoulders. 'My dear, there comes a time in many men's lives when they appear to—to resent their lost youth, and at such times they can do strange and most unwise things. I think perhaps your father has been lonely.'

'He has me and you and his books.'

'Perhaps it has not been enough.' She sighed. 'Rosa is very beautiful and spirited. And, as you know, you will shortly be leaving him when you marry Alvin. I expect he thinks of that.'

'But to *marry* her! Why did he not . . . not . . .'

Miss Flora's face turned rosy. 'My dear! Such a thing would never enter your father's head! He is a true gentleman and his actions have always been guided by the highest moral considerations.'

'Then I wish for once they had been lower!' Lalia cried, her eyes flashing. 'I wish he had taken her as a mistress—until he tired of her!'

'*Lalia*! Oh hush, you must not say such a thing!' Miss Flora exclaimed in agitated tones.

'But cannot you see it is impossible for it to be a successful marriage? A girl such as she will soon tire of life in a country house, she will want excitement and entertainment.'

'My dear, if she loves your father she will be happy just to be with him,' her aunt chided gently. 'It has been a great shock to us both, but we must accept the situation and make the best of it. At least it will mean your father will not miss you quite so much when you marry.'

'You mean that girl will take my place?' Lalia said bitterly. 'Perhaps she will—and perhaps she will not. She will make trouble, Aunt, for all of us. I know it, I can *feel* it! I—I think I hate her!'

'No, no, you shall not say such a wicked thing, my dearest Lalia! It will not be so long before you will leave us and start a new life with dear Alvin. Are you not being a little selfish? Does not your father's happiness matter to you?'

'Yes, if I thought this marriage would bring him happiness—but it won't, I am convinced of it.'

'We must make the best of it. I must see Mrs Grant, she must be told.'

'I've no doubt she already knows; and all the county will know and gossip and whisper and laugh! I shall ignore her. I refuse to see her take my place at the table tonight!'

But she was spared this as Rosa decided to dine in her room. After dinner Lalia took her father's coffee to him in the library.

'My deal child, I see how surprised you and my sister are,' he said, putting aside his cigar. 'I did not dream my letter of explanation had not reached you.'

'But Papa,' Lalia sank onto a little stool beside him, 'you did not, even in your last letter, mention any intention of marrying again, nor of your—your interest in Miss Carew.'

Her father smiled a trifle ruefully. 'I am afraid I am at fault there, my child. I found it difficult to write and express my feelings for Rosa, I am a reserved man at heart.'

'The marriage was so sudden.'

'Perhaps, but it seemed wise to us. Rosa's mother is not well-off, and she could not come to England; and she has four other daughters to care for, so we decided to get married in Spain. There were formalities, of course, but luckily I have some influence there, and Rosa is a British subject. Her father was in the army. He died some years ago and left his family sadly provided for.'

Naturally Mrs Carew was anxious to get one of her daughters married to a titled, wealthy husband, Lalia thought bitterly. How easily her father had been taken in; for the first time she realised he was essentially a weak man.

She slept badly that night and was aware of the avid curiosity in Nancy's eyes when she dressed her hair next morning. How soon would the news get around the neighbourhood? And how soon would visitors call to pay their respects to—and satisfy their curiosity about—the new mistress of Winterbridge Hall?

Rosa breakfasted in bed and did not come downstairs until shortly before lunch. Lalia, restlessly roaming about the house and hoping Alvin might come so she could pour out her distress to him, found her sitting before the library fire with a cashmere shawl around her shoulders.

She looked up as Lalia entered and called her to come and sit beside her. Lalia reluctantly obeyed.

Rosa did not beat about the bush. 'You are not pleased that I have married your Papa. You are shocked and perhaps unhappy because you did not know of it. It was unfortunate the letter was lost. But now I am here, you must accept that *I* am mistress of the house and that I am your step-mother.' She burst into laughter, her dark eyes sparkling. 'It is too stupid, is it not? I don't *look* like a step-mother and I certainly do not *feel* like one! Anyway, you will be marrying and leaving Winterbridge Hall so it would be better to stop being cross and accept me, wouldn't it?'

It was what Aunt Flora had suggested and Lalia knew it was the only sensible way to face the situation.

'Very well, Rosa,' she managed a smile as she said it.

'Now you are being sensible. Of course I shall take control of the household since I am mistress here, you know. You and your aunt can help me if you wish.'

'I am sure you will manage perfectly without us.'

Lalia studied the soft, oval face, creamy skin and liquid, dark eyes and full, sensuous mouth and wondered how long it would take for Rosa to become bored with household affairs. She was like a vividly-hued tropical bird who might find Winterbridge Hall a cage once the novelty had worn off.

'Of course, I shall not always be here,' Rosa remarked, as if guessing her thought. 'I am not fond of the country and Ashley has promised to take a house for me in London for the season.'

Lalia was in the morning-room when Alvin was shown in. She raised her face for his kiss and said, 'Alvin, you have heard the news?'

'Something of it. Surely it isn't true? Your father married to a young, half-Spanish girl? What can have driven him to such foolishness?'

'I do not know. It was the greatest shock to us. He had written, but we never received the letter. Alvin, it is a true disaster! She is so young, and rather beautiful in an exotic way. Papa appears devoted, but I cannot believe she married him for love. Her mother is poor, and there are other daughters.'

'And between them they lured your father into a marriage that may not prove happy for him.'

Lalia nodded unhappily. 'I cannot get used to the idea she is mistress here.'

'You do not have to,' he consoled her. 'Soon, you will have a house of your own; and perhaps your father will miss you less now he is married.'

'That is what Aunt Flora says—' she broke off as Rosa entered the room. She wore a dress of crimson silk trimmed with heavy guipure lace, much too elaborate for the occasion. The tight bodice showed off her seductive curves and the draped overskirt emphasised the lazy swing of her hips as she came across the room.

'This is your fiancé, Lalia? Please introduce me, I am most happy to meet him.' She held out her hand, her dark eyes alight with interest as they rested on Alvin's tall, upright figure and distinguished features. 'You did not tell me he was so handsome,' she laughed softly. 'Ah, now I make him embarrassed! I forget I am in England. You must teach me, Lalia, to be cool and reserved—though I do not know if you will succeed.'

'Please, don't try,' Alvin's glance, startled at first,

warmed as he smiled at her. 'A little Spanish gaiety will be good for us.'

Lalia had not missed the gleam in Rosa's eyes when Alvin smiled at her. Rosa would seek to enchant all men, it was her nature to demand admiration and flattery, she needed them as a flower needs water and without it she would droop. Lalia could almost feel pity for such a bright bird caged in a sombre old country mansion and something akin to anger rose inside her against her father who could not see it. She came out of her musings to hear Alvin remark,

'Lady Darrencourt likes to ride, you must find her a mount, Lalia.'

'Oh yes, I should like that very much,' Rosa exclaimed.

Lalia turned to Alvin. 'I have ordered the carriage as I want to visit Mrs Brookford and enquire how she does. Your cousin says she is to take treatment for her rheumatic condition.'

'I'll come back with you,' he said. To Rosa, watching them with speculative eyes, he said: 'My mother will call upon you once you are perfectly settled, Lady Darrencourt.'

'How kind,' Rosa brushed back a glossy curl. 'Do not forget I like to ride. I shall join you and Lalia on your gallops . . . if I am allowed to?' She glanced at Lalia who said stiffly,

'You will be very welcome.'

Alvin rode beside the carriage to Kingsweir. Lalia, glancing at him, thought how handsome he was with his fine profile, thick chestnut hair and military bearing. He met her eyes and his smile flashed out, lending an irresistible attraction to his face. No wonder Rosa tried her wiles upon him, Lalia reflected as she pulled her short fur cape around her. Despite the sunshine the wind was cold, as if winter were loath to release its hold upon the land.

Mrs Brookford, Romey's mother, was a tall, slender woman with a look of suffering on her face. She greeted Lalia warmly and said. 'Romey will be here shortly.'

'Are the treatments doing you good, Mrs Brookford?' Lalia asked.

Mrs Brookford sighed. 'I hope they will, but I fear the trouble is of long standing.'

When Romey came in he nodded to Alvin and seated himself beside Lalia and waited until he could ask, under cover of the conversation, 'How do you like your new step-mother? I hear she is very beautiful—and will take the reins of authority from you.'

'I advise you not to listen to gossip,' Lalia said sharply. 'I am only too pleased not to have to bother with household matters.'

'So you still like to pretend?' She disliked the mockery in his eyes extremely. 'I wondered if you would improve as you grew up.'

She stared at him indignantly. '*Improve*?'

'Yes,' he said deliberately, 'it was why I wanted to see you again.'

She waited, biting her lip and fidgeting with her gloves. At last her curiosity overcame her annoyance and she could not resist asking, 'And *have* I improved?'

He looked at her and again she saw that curious light in his eyes that had the power to disturb her self-possession.

'You've grown into a beauty,' his voice was quite impersonal, 'and you have developed your natural charm into something that is . . . rather potent. But you are still vain, selfish and cruel.'

She gasped and let her gloves fall to the ground as she rose swiftly.

'Thank you, Mr Brookford, I am charmed with your assessment of my character! But I will *not* allow I am cruel!'

'No?' he shrugged his shoulders. 'Isn't your treatment

of your Aunt Mildred and her two unfortunate daughters cruel? I think so.'

'You are impertinent!' she said furiously.

'I am truthful. Now you may hate me completely and forget the episode of the fishpond.' He picked up her gloves and she saw laughter in his eyes as he handed them to her. 'Perhaps I should have let you drown, but on the whole I'm glad I didn't.'

As Alvin handed her into the carriage she said abruptly: 'I don't like your cousin Romey.'

'Oh, he's all right. He speaks his mind in a way some people don't care for, and he never pretends to like anything he doesn't.'

'Well he does not like me, that is plain. Not that it matters in the least. Call for me tomorrow morning, Alvin, and we'll ride over the twenty acres.'

'Good—and find a horse for your step-mother; we've got to be friendly to her now she is here.'

'Yes, Rosa is here and I must put up with her,' Lalia thought as she was driven away. 'She probably *is* finding life a trifle strange here and there is no sense in antagonising her, and my father loves her. And when I am married to Alvin I can forget her!'

CHAPTER
THREE

In the days following the shock of Sir Ashley's marriage, Lalia slowly came to terms with the situation. She was certain her father had made an unhappy mistake, but it was too late to mend matters and little good would come of an open disagreement between herself and Rosa.

The first hint of trouble came when Mrs Grant, who had been housekeeper in the family since Lalia was born, resigned her position.

She stood before Lalia, a small, grey-haired Scotswoman whose arms had often comforted Lalia in childish troubles and whose devotion and loyalty to the family had never been questioned.

'I feel bad, Miss Lalia, indeed I do, it is like tearing my heart out to leave you,' her mouth quivered for a second before she went on, 'but now that things are changed, I find I'm not needed. There's new ways here, Miss Lalia, and I'm a body that can't change my ideas. I'd like to go at the end of the month if it's convenient.'

'Oh, Granty,' Lalia used her old childish name, 'you know it isn't convenient at all! We *can't* lose you! After all these years it is unthinkable! I know things have been . . . difficult lately, but I am sure Lady Darrencourt hasn't meant to upset you.'

'Mebbe no, but she *has*, Miss Lalia, and I can't abide interference with my work. Sir Ashley and Miss Flora and yourself have never complained—'

'Indeed no, Granty. I don't know what we would have done without you. You mustn't leave us now!'

'It's a bitter decision I've made, Miss Lalia dear, and I don't deny I've shed many a tear before I made it. But the truth is I cannot do my work properly under Lady Darrencourt's rule, so I'll go at the end of the month, please.'

Lalia sprang up and caught one of the wrinkled old hands that had so often wiped away childish tears.

'Granty, I won't let you go! Please stay until I marry, and then come with me to Kingsweir. As you know, Mrs Prior will be moving to the dower house and I will have the big house to manage. You *will* come, won't you? Truly, I shall need you. I would not have taken you from here, but if you intend to leave, that is different.'

The housekeeper's face relaxed in a happy smile. 'Oh, Miss Lalia, that would be just fine! I'd ask for nothing better. I'll stay here till you leave and let her ladyship have her fancy ways, though it's in my mind she'll tire of it before long.'

Her prophesy proved correct. In a few weeks, Rosa was complaining of her responsibilities and gradually Lalia took back the reins of the household.

Alvin had found a horse in his stables that suited Rosa, and the morning rides were now usually a threesome. Rosa was a confident but somewhat reckless rider. She led the way, her dark eyes brilliant and her glossy curls breaking loose as she rode over the parklands.

'Ah, this is wonderful!' Rosa cried. 'Come, Alvin, I will race you to the river.' She flung him a challenging glance.

Lalia followed more slowly, amused at her stepmother's need for constant attention. It amused Alvin too, she knew, when he supplied the gallant compliments so patently fished for and saw the full red lips curve seductively in a satisfied smile. Some of the neighbours had already called and Rosa had soon made it obvious where her interests lay. The women bored her and she left them to Lalia and her aunt, the men she gathered around her, flirting with her fan and using her magnificent eyes to good effect. Lady Grange had called and her daughters had gaped at Rosa's finery and confident manners.

'I confess I find it excessively strange that your father should have chosen so young a woman for his wife,' she murmured to Lalia as she sipped her tea. 'Half Spanish, I believe. You can see it, can't you? Quite *voluptuous*, that mingling of blood.'

'She is very beautiful,' Lalia answered, 'and my father is very happy, and so am I now I know he will not be lonely when I leave him.'

She escaped from the tea-party and ordered the pony-carriage and drove to Kingsweir where she found Alvin busy with his agent.

'I'm afraid I shall be occupied for a little time, my dear,' he said, 'but you will find Romey in the library.'

'I shall walk in the rose garden until you are free,' she told him. She had no intention of seeking out the man who had been so unjust in his assessment of her character and whose remarks, much to her irritation, continued to prick her like a hidden burr.

'Vain? Well, I *am* beautiful,' she told herself, 'and why should I pretend I am plain? Cruel . . . just because I do not enjoy the company of those silly girls!'

She crossed the lawn and stood looking down at a small pond where an occasional gleam of gold showed.

'Pray do not consider falling into it,' a voice said behind her, startling her. 'You are much too elegant a lady to be hauled out by your skirts now.'

The grass had deadened his footsteps and he was standing behind her.

'May I suggest you come away? The goldfish might be too great a temptation for you,' he said.

Against her will she laughed. 'You won't let me forget it, will you? I thought you were reading in the library.'

'I saw you pass the window.'

'And decided to come out and dissect my character even more brutally?'

He shook his head, a smile touching his mouth, a well-cut mouth, strong, stern and one that could be harsh, she thought, as she turned and walked beside him back to the path.

She enquired about his mother and he told her she did not feel the treatment she was receiving had done her any good and he was planning to take her back to Dorset.

'At least she has had a rest and change of air,' he said. 'I have been told by the doctor who attended her that there is a new type of treatment being practised by an Austrian doctor in London which is producing excellent results, although it is a slow process.' His dark brows drew together in a frown. 'But it is expensive . . . What a hell lack of money can be! People say money is a curse, that's a lie. It is the lack of money that is a wretched curse!'

Lalia was silent, made uncomfortable by the rough pain in his voice. She was relieved to see Alvin coming towards them.

'Mother would like to see you,' he said, slipping an arm around her waist, 'she is in the morning-room.'

Mrs Prior looked up from her desk when Lalia was shown in.

'Ah, my dear, I wanted to speak to you about your trip to London. I find I have to go there myself and I thought you might like to accompany me. We can stay with my brother who has a house in Berkeley Square and will be delighted to entertain us. You will be perfectly free to do all your shopping and we can return to Yorkshire together. How would that suit you?'

'Quite splendidly, thank you. My wedding dress is ordered, but I must have some fittings,' Lalia said. 'It is indeed kind of you to suggest it.'

Soon after this, Alvin joined them. When she stood with him on the front steps, waiting for her pony-carriage to be brought around, Lalia said, 'Alvin, will you sometimes ride with Rosa while I am away? She gets so bored on her own and my father has retreated to his library and his beloved books.' She sighed. 'He does not realise how much Rosa misses society and excitement. Flirt with her, Alvin dearest, and keep her vanity satisfied.'

'I'll do my best,' he assured her gaily.

He took Rosa out the day Lalia was busy with preparations for her journey to London and when they returned, Rosa demanded he accompany her the next day when she had to pay some return visits, since Sir Ashley had gently but firmly declined to go with her, saying he already knew all his neighbours and was not over fond of weak tea and gossip.

At last all was ready and Lalia and Mrs Prior, accompanied by Nancy, set off by the morning train for London.

Mrs Prior was not an interesting companion, she was somewhat shallow and much taken up with the importance of rank and wealth and Lalia let her prattle on about her London friends without paying much attention. Suddenly she heard her mother-in-law-to-be saying, with a little laugh, 'I fear your step-mother is getting herself talked about. I suppose it is her upbringing, and her foreign blood, that gives her that forward manner in society.'

'She was educated in England.'

'Well, her behaviour is certainly not English,' Mrs Prior said tartly, 'particularly with the *men*. I thought I would mention it to you, my dear, as you might be able to restrain her from making herself too conspicuous.'

'She is very young, and very beautiful.'

'Yes, *such* a pity,' Mrs Prior sighed, and fell to reading the *Illustrated London News*.

The visit to London proved more enjoyable than Lalia

expected. Mrs Prior's brother liked to entertain and there were dinner-parties and visits to the theatre and drives in the park.

'Monsieur Voizard admires you excessively, you know,' Mrs Prior remarked one morning, 'he was perfectly dismayed to know you were engaged to be married.'

'You mean that good-looking young Frenchman who took me in to dinner on Tuesday?' Lalia asked. 'I found him amusing, and very well informed on music and literature. Did you know he sent me flowers the next day?'

'But that is quite shocking! You are an engaged girl! He should not have done it!' Mrs Prior exclaimed.

Lalia laughed. 'Perhaps it is allowed in France. I was not at all offended, I assure you.'

She did not think it necessary to mention the note she had found inside the magnificent bouquet of lilac and roses. The man who had sent it had made it plain he admired her. Perhaps she should have repressed his ardent glances and ignored his compliments more pointedly, but he had been so charming, and it had made up a little for missing Alvin's attentions.

Mrs Prior wished to extend the visit by some days and Lalia had to agree. The wedding dress was complete down to the last lace-trimmed ruffle, an enchanting, pearl-trimmed dress for a fairy princess. With her mother's Limerick lace veil, pink roses and lily-of-the-valley for her bouquet and a retinue of pretty bridesmaids in pink, it would be a charming effect when the bright May sunshine fell upon them from the windows of the old Norman church.

There were two more theatre parties and a concert, at which Monsieur Voizard was present and usually to be found at Lalia's side. He was discreet, his attentions did not embarrass her, but she was aware his interest was deeper than it should have been for an engaged young lady.

On the journey back Mrs Prior became sentimental about the wedding.

'It is indeed the happiest event, my dear Lalia. Your dear mother and I always planned for you and my handsome Alvin to marry. He loves you most devotedly, you know.'

'So he tells me,' Lalia said, smiling. She felt warm and happy in the knowledge of that love—protecting, admiring and worshipping. How sad so few girls could know such happiness.

Her Aunt Flora welcomed her home in a twitter of agitation.

'Mrs Grant has been a tower of strength, Lalia—and the gardener says the flowers will be ready in time—but the extra champagne glasses have not arrived although ordered three weeks ago!'

'Do not worry, Aunt Flora,' Lalia bent to kiss her aunt's cheek, 'I am sure everything will go aright and the reception will be perfect. Things always go right for me you know, I was born under a lucky star.'

'Oh pray do not say so, it is not lucky, you know.' Miss Flora glanced around her and sank her voice to a conspiratorial whisper. 'I fear Rosa has *not* been helpful, in fact I have seen very little of her lately, she is out a great deal. She appears to have little interest in your wedding and I confess I am quite disappointed in her.'

Sir Ashley welcomed Lalia warmly, but Rosa did not put in an appearance until late in the afternoon and her manner was faintly constrained.

'Oh—did you have a pleasant trip?' She untied the strings of the wide straw hat she wore and stood glancing around her. Lalia observed Rosa was avoiding her eyes and was amused. What mischief had she been up to, she wondered? Flirting with the new curate?

A dozen questions awaited answers and a dozen problems needed to be solved and Lalia was plunged into consultations with Mrs Grant, her aunt and her father. The long ballroom had been cleared in preparation for the reception and rooms got ready for such guests as were staying the night. All was bustle and confusion and it was only late that night, when she was letting Nancy brush her hair, that she realised Alvin had not put in an appearance.

'Poor dear man,' she thought, 'he is frightened by all this fuss! I don't believe men *enjoy* their wedding, they would like to be cavemen and carry us off without ceremony.'

She drank the hot milk Nancy brought her and was soon sound asleep and dreaming of Italy where she and Alvin were to have their honeymoon. There were blue skies above her, but far on the horizon she could see a tiny black cloud appear and steadily grow larger . . . larger . . .

She awoke with a start. It was still early and the maid had not yet drawn the curtains. She lay for a time, her hands clasped behind her head, thinking of her new home and the changes she would make.

Suddenly she heard quick footsteps and a minute later Nancy burst into the room. Her startled expression made Lalia sit up and exclaim,

'Nancy, what is the matter?'

'Oh, Miss Lalia, I don't know exactly . . .'

Lalia sprang from her bed. 'Tell me at once what this is about!'

'All I knows, Miss Lalia, is that when Lady Darrencourt were called she weren't there—and her bed weren't slept in neither!'

'Not in her room?' Lalia pulled open the curtains and looked out at the dew-drenched lawns. A thin sunlight was fading before the advance of a lowering bank of cloud. Her dream came back to her and she shivered. 'What can have happened to her? Did she go out last night?'

She swung around to see her aunt in the doorway, her grey hair in curlpapers and partially concealed under a silk cap. She held her dressing-gown around her with one hand and in the other, a letter.

'Leave us, Nancy,' she said quietly, but Lalia heard the quiver in her voice and her nerves tightened, and when they were alone, she burst out.

'What is all this, Aunt Flora? Nancy says Rosa has not slept in her room!'

'Oh Lalia, my dearest child, I do not know anything— but I think you had better read this,' she held out the letter with a trembling hand, 'a groom from Kingsweir has just brought it.'

'From Kingsweir?' Lalia snatched the letter and opened it. As she read, her face grew deathly pale and she gave a cry of horror.

'Lalia, my child, what is it? Oh pray tell me what has happened!' her aunt implored.

Slowly Lalia raised her eyes; she looked stunned and her lips quivered as she whispered,

'They have gone—Alvin and Rosa! Eloped . . . they left last night . . . he is taking her to Jamaica, to his sugar estate there! They may be on the high seas by now!'

'Oh no!' Miss Flora cried. 'It isn't possible! She couldn't be so wicked! And Alvin, who loves you so truly!'

Lalia shook her head. 'No, Aunt, he loves Rosa, he says so. He begs my forgiveness . . . Oh!' she looked up, 'how shall I tell my poor father? What will this do to him?' She sank onto the bed, gripping Alvin's letter in hands that were suddenly icy. 'Aunt, you must help me to bear it! Alvin, and Rosa . . .' she turned to the window and saw the last rays of sunlight obliterated by dark cloud.

'It is true,' she thought dazedly, 'my sunlight is gone and the shadows have come at last!'

CHAPTER
FOUR

How cold it was! Lalia pulled her shawl around her shoulders and held her chilled hands to the fire. But perhaps it is only I who am cold, she thought. Shock chills the blood, they say.

Twilight was thickening shadows and turning colours to a uniform grey. A footman entered softly and lit the lamps, keeping his eyes averted from the still figure crouching over the fire.

They all know by now, of course, she thought, pressing her hands to her aching brow. The news would spread like wildfire, and all the county would know that Miss Lalia Darrencourt, heiress and acknowledged beauty, had been jilted a week before her wedding day! And that Sir Ashley's marriage had failed, as so many had prophesied in whispers, although no one had imagined in such a shameful fashion.

Sir Ashley had collapsed on hearing the news of his young wife's elopement with his future son-in-law and the doctor had been sent for and was with him now. Added to the shock of Alvin's treachery, Lalia now had grave fears about her father's condition. The doctor had been guarded; it was too early for a pronouncement. Sir Ashley must have rest, the shock had been very great and he was a delicate man.

Alvin and Rosa! Lalia's hands tightened in her lap as she stared into the bright flames. Why had she not suspected something? Why had she not noticed Rosa's growing interest in Alvin and realised how likely it was that a woman with Rosa's nature would tire all too soon of an elderly husband who already, Lalia suspected, had begun to realise his lack of wisdom in marrying her? Rosa was a woman with a strong sexual nature, she attracted men and was attracted by them. She had fallen in love with Alvin and he had not resisted her wiles. His letter, short to the point of brusqueness, was burned into her brain.

'I know what I do is beyond all forgiveness, but I cannot help myself. I cannot live without her . . . Forget me, Lalia.'

Forget their childish affection which had grown into love? Alvin had never looked at the girls who had lost their hearts to him, but Rosa, seductive in her dark beauty, had aroused in him a passion that took no heed of shameful desertion! Those days she had spent in London, was it then that they planned their flight?

Mrs Prior had written an incoherent letter laying all blame on Rosa, and had returned to London unable, Lalia guessed, to face the county's condemnation of her son's behaviour.

The door opened and Lalia looked up to see the doctor enter, followed by Miss Flora.

'What is it?' she whispered. 'Is Papa worse?'

'Sir Ashley has suffered a stroke, I fear,' the doctor spoke gently, his eyes on her blanched face. 'He will need careful nursing, I shall send a nurse, and I shall return tonight. I think you should rest, Miss Darrencourt, the strain is telling upon you. I will leave you a draught to help you sleep.'

'Oh, I cannot! Not while Papa is so ill.'

'But I do not wish you to become ill also, you need all your strength at a time like this.'

'But Papa—'

'We must hope for the best.'

Mrs Grant put her to bed and made her drink the

doctor's draught and sat beside her, softly stroking her hand until sleep claimed her. The old house had a hushed air, as if brooding on the events that had stricken down its master and destroyed the hopes of the girl who was once the envy of the county and who would now never be Alvin Prior's bride.

The days that followed had a nightmare quality for Lalia. Her father, cared for devotedly by the nurse, Miss Flora and herself, lay pale and weary and the doctor's face was grave when he visited him.

From somewhere the news came that Rosa and Alvin had sailed from Bristol on a steamship bound for one of the sugar ports. Lalia knew of Silverstone, the Prior sugar estate in the colony. Alvin had talked of it and his visit to the estate after his father had died and he had become owner. He had liked the colourful island and no doubt Rosa had thought it sounded romantic. There would be no attempt to follow and persuade them to return, the shame and distress the two lovers had brought on their families made them outcasts. Beneath her grief for her father, Lalia felt a burning anger; if her father died, Rosa and Alvin would be responsible for his death!

On going into her father's room one morning Lalia was startled to see Romey sitting by the bed. He rose as she approached.

'I called to enquire how Sir Ashley did,' he said, 'and it seems he expressed a wish to see me.'

'The doctor is the only man I see now,' Sir Ashley grumbled. 'Romey has been telling me of his stables in Dorset and how he has had to sell some of the horses, a bad business.'

'Not so bad, sir,' Romey said, 'I got a good price for them. I must go—'

'No, please stay,' Lalia said quickly, 'I can see Papa is enjoying your visit.'

She retreated to the library; she had no wish to meet

Romey again, but he sought her out.

'Your father is more cheerful than I expected,' he said abruptly, after she had perforce invited him to take a seat, 'but you look unwell.' His eyes took in her pale face and listless air. 'This has been a most unhappy affair. Alvin was always weak, but I had not expected this of him.'

'I—I do not wish to speak of it,' she said stiffly, keeping her eyes on her hands folded in the lap of her grey cashmere gown.

'Alvin was never worthy of you. Rosa twined him around her finger, she is a woman who lives by her instincts, her sexual desires.'

'Stop! I refuse to listen to you!'

'Face the truth, Lalia. Alvin eloped with Rosa because he felt passion for the first time in his life. She aroused him in a way no other woman had. You are deeply concerned about the effect this has had on your father, but for yourself, some of your distress is the humiliation of your unpleasant position as a deserted bride.'

She sprang to her feet, hot colour flooding her face.

'You are outrageous! How dare you speak to me so? I won't listen to you! Leave me!'

'Very well.' He regarded her for a moment, his eyes speculative. 'At least I've aroused you to some sign of life, you looked depressingly funereal. Believe me, I am sorry—'

'I do not want your sorrow!' she flung at him.

He walked to the door and turned. 'You're right, you have enough sorrow of your own, sorrow for your father—but not so very much for Alvin,' his eyes were too perceptive for her liking. 'You have not wept for him.' He bowed and left her.

She stood, her hands clenched and cheeks fiery. How had he known that she had not shed tears for Alvin? Shock, horror at such treachery, bitterness at trust betrayed, anger . . . she had felt all these, she knew. But sorrow?

'I have felt too deeply for tears,' she told herself quickly. 'I won't let Romey come again.'

But he came because Sir Ashley asked for him. The Brookfords had stayed on at Kingsweir to look after the house while Mrs Prior recovered from the shock of her son's flight.

A few people called to express condolence at Sir Ashley's illness and Lalia let her aunt receive them. She guessed it was as much curiosity as concern that brought people to the house and she had no intention of braving spiteful glances and obliquely worded sympathy for her unhappy situation, a situation that would cause unkind amusement and possible satisfaction among some of the families she had so carelessly treated in the past. She grew hot at the thought of all that was being said and thought about her and even the pity of kinder souls was abhorrent. As soon as her father was better, she would take him away to the sea, or abroad.

But, with a sinking heart, she realised that Sir Ashley was not getting better. He grew weaker day by day and she knew that his hold on life was growing frailer. She gathered courage to ask the doctor his opinion.

'You will have to be brave, my dear Miss Darrencourt,' the pity she saw in his eyes struck dread into her heart. 'He does not suffer, but there is no desire to live, his spirit is gone, I fear. It cannot be long now.'

It came suddenly, ten days later. A gentle slipping out of a world that had lost its charm for him. Sir Ashley Darrencourt of Winterbridge Hall died in his sleep on the last day of May, a soft sunny day when trees shook out their fresh greenery and hedgerows were snowy with hawthorn blossom and the world seemed full of a joy that could not heal Lalia's hurt. At last the tears came, and life seemed black indeed. She sorrowed for her father and for herself. Now she was alone, her aunt, suddenly aged by strain and sorrow, had become feeble and needed attention. The house grew silent, as if it too mourned the dead, and Lalia, moving restlessly about it in her black gown, knew a bleakness of spirit such as she had never imagined could be hers.

The funeral took place and was attended by friends and relations. Mrs Prior, deeply veiled, took Lalia aside.

'My poor child, so terrible a loss following Alvin's desertion! What will you do now? Will you stay here?'

'I do not know,' Lalia said wearily. 'My aunt is unwell and finds Winterbridge Hall too full of memories to wish to remain with me.'

'But you *must* have someone. I wish I could be of help, but my wretched nerves make me perfectly helpless! My doctor says it is imperative I spend some time abroad and I plan to visit friends in the south of France. Oh, if only your poor father had not married that creature! She bewitched my dearest Alvin, I am convinced of it! He always loved you, Lalia, since you were children together. He will tire of her.'

'It is very probable he will marry her now,' Lalia said, 'since she is free to do so.'

'Oh! My poor unfortunate Alvin!' Obviously such an idea had not entered Mrs Prior's head. 'It will ruin him!'

Some days later Lady Grange and her daughters called, ostensibly to offer condolences.

'Such a terrible time for you, my poor Lalia,' her aunt murmured, 'and with Flora keeping to her bed and being of no use to you. Of course, Ashley was never strong and the shock of his wife's elopement hastened his death, I fear. I truly pity your situation, dear Lalia.'

'Such a *very* different situation from when we last met,' Harriet said, her eyes spiteful as she stared at Lalia, pale and composed in her black dress. 'Such shameful behaviour of Alvin's, abandoning you for that woman just a week before your wedding! With your wedding dress and bridesmaids chosen—'

Lady Grange had the grace to look ashamed. She said sharply, 'That is enough, Harriet.'

But Harriet's face was suddenly blotched with unbecoming red as she burst out. 'Perhaps it is a judgment on her because of her treatment of us! To despise us, never to ask us to parties or balls—'

'Oh Harriet, pray hush!' Nina implored.

'Harriet, I am ashamed of you! Come, it is time we left.' Lady Grange swept her daughters before her out of the room.

Left alone, Lalia sat staring into the fire. So that was how everyone saw her, the girl Alvin had thrown over and whose pride was in the dust! That she deserved her downfall because she had been too proud in her beauty and happiness!

'I won't stay! I—I cannot face them all!' She sprang to her feet just as the footman announced: 'Mr Brookford.'

He crossed the room swiftly. 'I saw the Grange carriage leaving. So they've been to crow? Don't tell me, your face has already done that. I'm afraid there will be others; human nature is cruel.'

'I shall go away.' She did not look at him.

'Please sit down, I want to talk to you. Now Mrs Prior is back, I shall be returning with my mother to Dorset.'

Reluctantly she sat down. 'Did you come to tell me that?'

'No. I've waited until I thought you had got over your father's death somewhat. I am glad to see you looking better, but you are too thin. Are you eating enough?'

She said, suddenly impatient: 'Is that what you have come to ask me?'

He shook his head. 'No. I've come to ask you to marry me!'

CHAPTER
FIVE

For a moment Lalia was too astounded to speak.

'You must be mad!' she stammered, 'or is this some kind of unpleasant joke?'

'I am not mad and it is not a joke.' He spoke calmly, almost casually. 'I expected you to be surprised. It is too soon, I know, but I'm off to Dorset in the near future which is why I'm speaking now, it will give you time to think it over.'

'You *must* be mad! To speak of such a thing—and at such a time as this!' She put her hand to her cheek and felt it burning. 'There is no possible reason for even thinking such a thing!'

'There are reasons, and one of them is that I need money.'

She stared at him, unable to believe what she had heard.

He went on, apparently unaware of the anger gathering in her eyes. 'My father left crippling debts that have to be paid. The estate needs money if it is not to go to ruin. If I sell it now I will not get a decent price for it, but money would bring it back to what it was before my father drained everything out of it. And there is my mother; she needs special treatment and I cannot afford it. The estate once paid well and it will again, if I do something *now*.'

Lalia waited until she could control her voice. Hot anger, disgust and resentment filled her so that she had difficulty in finding words.

'You put your case well, but has it not struck you—or

are you too sunk in selfish consideration of *your* needs—
that *I* am involved in all this, as well as my fortune?'

'Very much so.' He sat back, watching her as she sat,
scarlet-cheeked, her eyes blazing and her slim figure taut
under the black gown with its relieving touches of white at
neck and wrist. 'You have suffered greatly. I know how
dear your father was to you and how you miss him, and
Alvin's cruel behaviour has hurt your pride as well as your
heart and brought you humiliation you find hard to bear.
You will not find life easy if you remain in Yorkshire
where people know your position. You are wealthy and
will have many suitors—'

'I shall never marry, *never*!' she declared passionately.

'I suggest you marry me. I can offer you an honourable
name and the not-to-be-despised status of a married
woman. You will have the chance to live in another part of
England, and you will be free to live your own life. I ask no
more of you than you take my name.'

'And bring you my fortune.'

'Yes,' he agreed. 'We do not really dislike each other,
you know, and we could easily become good friends. If
you could interest yourself in bettering conditions for my
tenants, I would be grateful. My mother has become very
fond of you and will make you welcome. You say you do
not mean to marry; I take it you mean marry for love.
Very well, marry for companionship, for security and
friendship.'

She rose and held out her hand. She was pale and there
was a trace of bitterness in the faint smile hovering around
her mouth.

'Goodbye, Romey. I truly believe you think such a
marriage would be successful; I must differ. You are
right, I do not dislike you and I appreciate your kindness
to my father before he died. But such a marriage is out of
the question.'

He stood looking at her, his expression giving her no

clue to his thoughts. Was he disappointed? Surely he could not have expected her—or any woman—to accept such a blunt, businesslike proposal? Her money in exchange for the security of marriage, even though a marriage in name only.

'I'll come again,' he said. 'I've put things rather brutally, but I'm afraid that is my way.' He bowed and left her.

Lalia sank back into her chair, prey to a medley of emotions that defied analysis. He would marry her for her fortune! And to be so frank about it! And yet . . . at least he had not tried to pretend he loved her. He knew she had done with love; love had betrayed her tragically. She sprang to her feet, too restless to remain still.

Why had she been so cruelly treated? Why had her life, so rich and secure, suddenly darkened until she felt the wings of fear beating close to her? She was alone, even Aunt Flora had failed her and was declaring the house was now haunted for her and she must leave.

She turned as James, the butler, opened the door and announced, 'Mr Ransome, the lawyer, is here Madam.'

'Please show him in, and tell Mrs Grant to see his room is prepared, he will be staying a few days to see to my father's affairs.'

Mr Ransome, small, dry and wise in the ways of his profession, had been the family lawyer for many years. He advanced on Lalia and shook her hand briefly as he said, 'This is a sad occasion, Miss Darrencourt. A great shock to us all. May I offer my most sincere sympathy?'

He took the chair she offered and refused her offer to order tea. His businesslike manner helped her to pull herself together and she tried to concentrate on all he had to say of her father's will and the provisions he had made for her.

'There is one point I must raise, Mr Ransome,' she said.

'Can my step-mother make any claim on the estate or such money as my father has left me?'

Mr Ransome pursed his lips thoughtfully, then slowly shook his head.

'She would be most unwise to attempt such a thing. Sir Ashley has made it perfectly plain she is to inherit nothing by his expressed wish. If she wanted to, she could try to contest the will, but in the—er—circumstances it is highly unlikely she would succeed.'

'Thank you. Please feel free to go through such of my father's papers and accounts as you wish. James will show you his study, please ring if you require anything.'

Miss Flora, who had declined to come down to dinner, said fretfully, 'I never could take to legal gentlemen, they *bother* me. Lalia, my dear, I feel I shall never recover my health here after all that has happened. The shock of Rosa and Alvin . . . my poor brother's death . . . I find myself in a sad state and should like to visit my sister who lives in Lowestoft. She says the air is extremely invigorating and invites me to pay a long visit.'

'Then you shall certainly go,' Lalia said, her heart sinking. Aunt Flora had been so much a part of her life that it would seem strange to be without her. She had aged greatly since her brother's death and her gentle mind was full of fears and frights. It was better that she should leave Winterbridge Hall.

For the next few days Mr Ransome was busy in Sir Ashley's study, working his way through many years of accounts, papers and letters, while Lalia arranged for her aunt to travel to Lowestoft. The heavy weight of grief at her father's death seemed added to by her aunt's imminent departure and the future seemed bleak indeed.

'You will not find life easy . . .' Romey's words came back to her and brought with them memory of their last meeting. He had not called again, possibly because he realised he had insulted her. But perhaps he had not precisely insulted her. He had made her an offer of marriage and been completely honest about his reasons for doing so. And he had not expected her to love him or pretended he felt love for her. Alvin had said he loved her . . . Quickly she put the thought from her. She would never trust a man's declared love again.

On his last day Mr Ransome came to her. 'I found, hidden in your father's bible, a letter addressed to you, Miss Darrencourt.' He gave her the envelope. 'It was quite by chance I found it, he must have put it there when he was stricken, perhaps shortly before he died. It could have remained there for years.'

Tears sprang to Lalia's eyes. She had bravely striven to adjust herself to losing her father, but this reminder of him brought a wave of emotion she could not control. She took the letter to her room and, brushing away the tears that blinded her, opened it and read the few short lines written so unevenly she had difficulty in deciphering them.

'Do not grieve for me, dearest daughter. I have no wish to live. But I am gravely worried that I do not leave you safe in a happy marriage. It is my dearest wish that you should marry Jerome Brookford. I have come to know him and he is a man to trust, an honourable and good-hearted man, unlike his cousin Alvin in every respect. He has asked my permission to address you and I have given it. Marry him, dearest Lalia, and you will have my blessing.'

She let the letter slip from her fingers. Romey had spoken to her father and asked his consent and obtained it! Had he been as frank as he had been with her, she wondered? Surely her father would be as contemptuous as she was with the idea she was being proposed to because she was an heiress? Even if Romey had not given his reasons, her father knew of Romey's burden of debts and the demands of his estate; and yet he would give her his blessing if she married him!

A maid knocked and was told to enter. 'Lady Grange and two young ladies, Mrs Grey and Mrs Clarkson and Miss Brown have called, Miss Lalia.'

So the vultures were gathering! Lalia shrank back.

'Tell them I am not receiving visitors yet.'

Perhaps it was a sincere wish to express sympathy, she thought wearily, but she could not be sure. She would never again be sure that a spiteful satisfaction at her unhappy state—the jilted bride—had not prompted such visits.

'I shall always suspect them,' she thought. 'I can't stay here, I am beginning to hate the county, the people— even this house!'

She heard carriage wheels on the front gravel, then all was silent. She picked up her father's letter and folded it carefully before putting it away. As she left her room she saw the footman coming up the stairs.

'Mr Brookford has called, Madam. Shall I say you are not at home?'

She hesitated for a moment. 'No, show Mr Brookford into the library.'

She walked to the looking-glass and stood, tall and slim in her black dress, studying herself. Her eyes, though still shadowed, were brighter and her face more resolute and she became aware for the first time of a stirring of renewed life within her, as if she were awakening from a long nightmare. She welcomed it although she did not understand it. Tucking a strand of hair in place, she went down to the library.

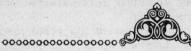

CHAPTER
SIX

ROMEY was looking out of the window when she entered. He swung around at the sound of her skirt rustling across the carpet and held out his hand.

'You look better,' he said, holding her hand in a firm, warm clasp. 'I hear your aunt is to leave you for a while.'

'Yes.' She let her hand rest in his for a moment before drawing it away. 'I do not think she will return to Winterbridge Hall.'

'Will you remain here alone?'

'I haven't made up my mind yet. I may go to London, after I have answered all the letters.'

She thought of one, unexpected, letter. Monsieur Voizard expressed his sympathy in words that could not offend and she had been pleased to hear from him. It brought back, for a moment, the carefree days she had spent in London. But now she had something else on her mind.

'Romey,' she met his eyes squarely, 'I did not know you had spoken to my father about . . . about . . .'

'About asking you to marry me? Yes, I did.'

'You did not tell me . . .' Suddenly, she knew why. He had no intention of using her father's permission to persuade her to accept him. How like him, she thought, to refuse any help. What he did, he did alone. Such self-confidence was probably a fault, yet she remembered as a child secretly admiring Alvin's sturdy, black-browed cousin who knew his own mind and steadily resisted pressure from authority if he thought it unfair, and the memory brought a sudden smile.

'So you can still smile,' he exclaimed. 'Sit down here and talk to me, Lalia. Have you fallen in any ponds lately?'

She shook her head as she seated herself beside him. 'You have my permission to count the goldfish. Romey, has there been news of . . . them?'

'No. He may have written to his mother. The sugar estate is a pretty large one, I believe, and he'll have his hands full managing it.'

'Do you think Rosa knows about my father?'

'I imagine the news will have reached her somehow.'

She looked down at her clasped hands. 'I suppose Alvin will marry her now.'

He did not answer. He looked preoccupied and suddenly jumping up he began to pace the room, frowning thoughtfully. She watched him, thinking how unlike the cousins were. Alvin's tall, slim figure, handsome features and gay charm marked him out in any company. At first people would not notice Romey's broad shoulders and muscular build or, in spite of them, how lightly and swiftly he could act when he wished. His features were strong rather than handsome, a high-bridged nose, uncompromising jaw and mouth and deep-set, darkly blue eyes.

He turned suddenly and caught her watching him. 'Well, what is the verdict?'

She felt herself blush and was annoyed. 'I was thinking that you and Alvin are very different.'

'As far as looks go, that isn't a compliment, you unkind creature. However, so far I have not lost my heart to any half-Spanish seductress.'

'Have you ever lost your heart to anyone?' she tilted her head to look up at him and saw his expression alter.

'How like a woman to ask that. Now, when are you going to marry me?'

She surprised herself by laughing. 'Don't be ridiculous! I am not marrying you.'

'Don't be so sure. I'll make an excellent husband. There will be no pretence we adore each other—I ask nothing but friendship from you, Lalia, and I shall never ask more, I promise you. But I shall look after you—and you need looking after. And if my mother can be cured, I will be forever grateful.'

'You love her, don't you?' she asked softly.

'She is all I have,' he said shortly, turning away, 'and her life has never been easy. Much of her complaint comes from years of great anxiety and privation and I would do much to make it up to her.'

And use my money to do it, Lalia thought, but without resentment. For the first time she had seen something approaching softness in Romey's face and it affected her oddly. Yes, he might make an excellent husband, but not for her, of course.

When he left her she sat for a long time, watching the shadows creep across the long lawns sweeping down to where the river reflected the last burning rays of the sun. Moths came out to dance and busy rustling and cheeping from the shrubbery told of birds settling down for the night.

If she married Romey she could move away from a neighbourhood where Alvin's desertion was food for gossip. She would have a home and the protection of a husband and the company of a woman she had grown to admire and who was prepared to welcome her as daughter-in-law. It might be interesting, too, to help in refurbishing a house, and put an estate in working order and so bring in an income to the Brookford family again. There could be worse ways of using the fortune her father had left her.

'It is my dearest wish that you marry Jerome Brookford . . . he is a man to trust . . . marry him, dearest Lalia, and you will have my blessing.' Her father had written that shortly before dying.

To marry without love; how she would have rejected that once! Now, she was done with love. Alvin had loved her, but his love had been weak in the face of temptation, as all love was weak. She had lost faith in love; it was not for her.

Why then, a small voice somewhere inside her asked, did she not accept Romey's offer and make her life in Dorset? Her few relations had shown no signs of interest in her, and she was growing to dread the thought of living in a house that held so many memories for her, and to be so near Kingsweir filled her with dismay. Mrs Prior would not let her forget the unhappiness and shame Alvin had brought them both. Yes, it was impossible to remain in Winterbridge Hall.

Aunt Flora went off, amid many protestations of affection, to Lowestoft and the house had a hollow ring when Lalia returned from seeing her into the train. She was surprised at her feeling of pleasure when she saw, from the parlour window, a horseman ride up to the house and hand his mare to a groom before running up the steps.

'I've come to take you to spend a few days at Kingsweir,' Romey said without preamble. 'You will be missing your aunt here, and my mother is feeling rather down and would be grateful for some company. Come, tell your maid to pack what you need and I'll order the carriage for you.'

'Romey, you are positively a highwayman,' she exclaimed, 'you would abduct me!'

'That's an idea. You'll only mope if I leave you here.'

For a moment she wavered. He had no right to order her about like this, yet she probably *would* mope if left alone. The pain of losing her father was still with her and

there were so many things around her that brought
memories. Suddenly she made up her mind.

'Very well, I will come, but only for one night.'

'Three nights. We don't leave for Dorset until Mon-
day.'

In a surprisingly short time her valise was packed and
she was being driven down the avenue with Romey riding
beside her.

Mrs Brookford kissed her warmly. 'My dear, this is
very good of you, just the sight of your pretty face has
cheered me. I fear Romey has found me poor company
lately. Sit down and tell me what you plan to do. I believe
your aunt is off to visit her sister?'

That evening, when she went to dress, Lalia found a
cluster of white roses on her table and knew Romey had
ordered them. Her dress of black silk was plain as a
mourning dress should be, the neck outlined with a
narrow silver ribbon and soft chiffon frills falling from the
elbow sleeves. She pinned the cluster of roses into the
front of the bodice before she went down to dinner.

The evening proved a pleasant one and for a time the
shadows receded and an unexpected brightness of spirits
claimed her. Mrs Brookford was looking better, with a
faint colour in her cheeks, and the three of them played
cards until the footman brought in tea at ten o'clock.

Romey had ordered a horse to be saddled and ready for
her after breakfast and together they rode to the wide
heathlands lying to the south of the estate. The air was
warm with promise of greater heat later as the sun gained
strength, and a faint haze made distances blurred and
mysterious. Lalia felt the first touch of happiness since
tragedy had entered her life as she galloped across the
springy turf.

In the afternoon Romey drove his mother and Lalia to
see a Summer Fair at a village.

'I know you are in mourning, my dear,' Mrs Brookford

said, 'but this could not be construed as going into society. I have always felt mourning, and especially the wearing of black, an unhappy custom. Would your father have wished it?'

Lalia shook her head. 'He never allowed me to wear black, he said it depressed him. He liked me to wear light, fresh colours, but one must take note of custom, alas.'

She was amazed to find time passing so pleasantly and swiftly. Romey was often at her side and she was grateful to him for the trouble he took to entertain her. Sometimes they argued, she protesting at his forthright opinions and his masculine assumption of authority.

'Women are no longer chattels,' she told him firmly, 'we can have careers of our own, and one day we may have the vote.'

'Mr Gladstone did not think so when he threw out Bright's suffrage bill on its second reading.'

'But now women have their own colleges and better education, he will not be able to stop us. Women will become doctors and lawyers and—'

'And the majority will become wives and mothers, which is their proper sphere.'

She began to protest, then saw he was laughing. She knew him better now, but he could—and often did—surprise her. She had been a trifle surprised, and piqued, that he had said nothing more of his proposal of marriage. Perhaps he had thought the better of it, or had taken her refusal as her final word—as of course it was, she assured herself quickly. She realised she would miss him when he left Kingsweir. He was a pleasant companion and she found many of his ideas stimulating. He spoke of what he hoped to do for his workers whose dwellings had been allowed to sink into a terrible condition, and of the saw-mill which had been a source of income, and the smooth grassy hills that had once supported the hardy Dorset sheep.

He drove her back to Winterbridge Hall and said: 'I'll call again to bid you goodbye,' before he left her.

How cold and bleak the house appeared to her. Her father's spirit, sad and disappointed, seemed to haunt the rooms. This was no longer her home, Lalia thought unhappily; perhaps it had ceased to be ever since Rosa had burst into her life.

Two days later Romey came again. As he entered the morning-room where she sat idle before her tapestry work she rose to greet him.

'So we are to say goodbye, Romey?' She was startled at the comfort she felt in his strong hand clasp. 'I—I shall miss you.'

'I am glad to hear it.'

'Will you be visiting Mrs Prior again?'

He shook his head. 'No. She is given too much to complaining of her woes. You will do well to avoid her, she'll make you the scapegoat rather than put any blame on her adored Alvin.'

She glanced at him uncertainly. Was he going without any allusion to his offer? Had he regretted it?

As he turned to go, the words came of their own accord before she could think, or control them: 'Romey, do you still want to marry me?'

He swung around, his eyes searching her face. 'Yes.'

'Without—love?'

'With friendship, respect and affection.'

I am mad! she thought. I *must* be! It can never succeed! He has said he wants my money . . . What do I want? I want kindness, freedom from the past, companionship, security.

In a voice strange to her ears she said: 'Very well, Romey, I have thought it over and I will marry you as soon as you wish.'

The wedding was in the little Norman church on the estate

in Dorset. As Romey had insisted she should not wear black, Lalia had chosen a soft grey gown trimmed with creamy lace. The roses he sent her were a deep, rich yellow, not the white she expected. She had hesitated for a moment, then pinned the roses on her dress and made a small bouquet to hold. Golden roses for a golden bride, she thought wryly, a bride who brought her husband gold. Well, she had made her choice and now there was no going back. In an hour she would be Mrs Jerome Brookford of Hildon Manor in the county of Dorset. It was a new life, untouched by past tragedies. The shadows were retreating and soon the sun would fill her world again. Romey would never ask more of her than she was prepared to give. She had obeyed her father's last wishes, and she had his blessing. And she was no longer an object of false sympathy and sly satisfaction, a bride forsaken by a faithless lover.

As they drove away from the church she looked about her with interest. It was the first time she had seen her new home and she was dismayed at the signs of neglect, the empty fields, broken fences, ill-kept woods and copses, and the condition of the labourers' cottages.

'Surely people cannot live in such hovels?' she exclaimed. 'There is one with a great hole in the roof!'

'People are obliged to,' he answered grimly. 'Families with four or six children live in them and get fevers from the ill-drained land around them. With the help of your money, Lalia, I can cure much suffering and hardship among my workers and tenants. Tell me, do you regret what you have done?'

She looked down at the ring on her finger. A golden ring for a golden bride. Did she regret it? She turned to see him watching her with a strange expression. 'No, I do not regret it,' she said slowly, and let her hand touch his for a moment.

CHAPTER
SEVEN

'PEOPLE may not call yet,' Mrs Brookford said as she and Lalia sat on the terrace of Hildon Manor, enjoying the warm July sunshine, 'since you are still in mourning. But I have asked our friends, the Overtons, to call as they are old friends and I am sure you will like them. Mrs Overton is a charming woman who does much good among the poor, and her two daughters could be pleasant companions for you, perhaps. Mr Overton was in the diplomatic service and is now retired, and there is a son, Malcolm, who was in the army, but now manages his father's estate.'

'I should like to meet them,' Lalia assured her.

The days seemed to have slipped by like a dream since her marriage. The house, shabby though it was, had a charm for her. It did not have the size and dignity of Winterbridge Hall, but there was a graciousness in the rooms that seemed always filled with sunshine. The neglected gardens with their sweet-scented roses, straggling wallflowers and flourishing crop of weeds had an appeal for her that she had not felt for the well-kept gardens of her former home, and strolling along the mossy paths, listening to the liquid notes of a blackbird and watching butterflies fanning their wings in the sun, she thought: 'I was right to marry Romey. I can be happy here.'

On Mr Ransome's advice she had rented Winterbridge Hall to a wealthy American family. She had brought Mrs

Grant and James the butler with her and they had settled comfortably into their new positions.

She did not see much of Romey, he was out early, riding over the estate, interviewing his agent, farmers and tenants and often did not return until late. If Mrs Brookford was aware of the nature of the marriage, she said nothing and willingly handed over the household management to Lalia.

Mrs Prior had not returned to Yorkshire. Her letter, written from London, had been a bitter condemnation of Lalia's behaviour in marrying while still in mourning and for so soon forgetting her love for Alvin. She would deeply regret it, Mrs Prior wrote. Romey wanted only her money, and the letter ended in a wild denunciation of Lalia's treatment of Alvin. If she had cared enough for him to see he was not exposed to Rosa's wicked desires the elopement would never have taken place.

Lalia threw the letter aside. So Romey was right, she was to be the scapegoat! How thankful she was she had moved from the sphere of Mrs Prior's rancour.

When the Overton family called, Lalia was at once attracted to them. Their welcome was sincere with no overtones of curiosity. Mrs Overton, a handsome woman who had been a beauty in her day, assured Lalia that her two daughters, Violet and Fanny, had been longing to meet her.

'I hear you like to ride,' she said, smiling, 'so you have that in common with Violet.'

'My brother Malcolm is always busy and refuses to ride with me,' Violet complained.

She was a pretty bright-eyed girl with soft brown hair and a gentle manner that pleased Lalia. Her sister, Fanny, had less charm and a somewhat pert air.

Before she left, Mrs Overton invited Lalia to tea the following week. That evening Lalia told Romey of the visit.

'I thought you would like them,' he said. 'Violet Overton is a sensible girl with a mind of her own. Fanny is a silly little flirt who will give her parents trouble one day.'

Lalia glanced at him as he sat idly stroking the ears of the old spaniel beside him.

'Did she ever try to flirt with you, Romey?'

He grinned. 'She tried to, but I'm afraid she found it hard work.'

'She was brave to attempt it,' she said, smiling down at the sewing in her lap.

'You don't think I'm worth flirting with? Perhaps you are right; I was never a ladies' man.'

She had a sudden memory of her question: 'Were you ever in love?' and the abrupt blankness that had shuttered his face. Was there a romance hidden in his past? Although he did not have Alvin's looks and charm, many women might well find him attractive in the very bluntness of his manner and his strong masculinity.

She looked up to see him watching her. He said abruptly, 'Are you happy? Don't try to spare my feelings, I want the truth.'

She looked at him thoughtfully for a minute. 'And what if I said I deeply regretted marrying you and was completely miserable?'

'I wouldn't believe you, you look better than you have for a long time. But I heartily dislike your black and grey dresses. Must you wear them?'

'It is the custom . . . but I admit I find them rather depressing. I think I will have a lavender dress made for me in Dorchester. Will that suit you?'

'It will be better than black,' he said, getting up, 'but I want to see you in rose colour.'

'My father liked me in that colour,' she murmured. 'I still have the rose evening dress he particularly liked.'

'Wear it one evening for me, Mama will not object, I know.' He straightened his shoulders as if weary. 'You must excuse me, my head shepherd awaits me. I mean to see our hills filled with Dorset sheep once again, they used to bring in a good income once.'

'But you have been working all day,' she protested.

'So you noticed it? It is a wifely concern I appreciate.' He put his hand under her chin, tilting her face to his. 'You were a pretty child and now you are a very beautiful young woman. I count myself lucky, in more ways than one. We're good friends, Lalia?'

'Good friends,' she said steadily, meeting his eyes. 'Romey, can I come with you when you inspect your workers' cottages?'

'Of course, if you want to. I didn't know such things interested you.'

'Perhaps you do not know me very well,' she said, and wondered, with a faint stir of uneasiness, just how well she knew this dark-browed man she had so abruptly married.

The Overtons lived in Stonewell Court, a modern, comfortable house with well-kept gardens and a small lake that was as blue as the sky above it when Lalia drove up in the open landau. Mrs Overton made her welcome and the girls, pretty in their light summer dresses of printed muslin, were obviously pleased to see her. As tea was brought in by a maid, a tall, slim young man appeared at the french window.

'This is my son, Malcolm,' Mrs Overton said with motherly pride.

'I have told Malcolm you promised to ride with me some mornings, Mrs Brookford,' Violet said. '*He* never has time, and Fanny has no spirit for a gallop.'

Fanny tossed her head. 'I get rumpled and untidy when I ride, and my horse never behaves well.'

Lalia noticed how intent the young man's eyes were and saw the colour rise in his cheeks as he said quickly, 'Oh, I'm not so busy now. I hope, Mrs Brookford, that I may be allowed to accompany you and my sister.'

'Good gracious!' Violet exclaimed. 'What a change! If Mrs Brookford agrees—'

'Oh, I shall be pleased,' Lalia assured her demurely. She had not missed the startled admiration in the young man's eyes and his changed attitude to morning riding amused her.

He sat beside her at tea and assiduously kept her supplied with bread-and-butter and seed cake.

Lalia liked his frank open manner. He was good-looking, with a manliness in his features, and his movements were quick and graceful. She did not dislike his homage to her beauty and it amused her vanity to know she had made a conquest.

'And how is dear Mrs Brookford?' Mrs Overton asked anxiously. 'I fear the treatment at Harrogate did her little good.'

'I am afraid that is true,' Lalia told her. 'I am planning to take her to London soon to try treatment by a Viennese doctor who has opened a clinic there.'

'I have heard very good reports of it and I pray it will bring relief to your mother-in-law.'

When Lalia left, Malcolm accompanied her to her carriage. He asked if she intended to ride with his sister the next morning and on being told such a plan had been arranged, asked permission to ride with them.

'Perhaps I ought not to feel flattered,' she thought as she was driven away, 'but I like him—and of course I have no intention of flirting with him, nor he with me.'

The next morning dawned mistily with a pale sun slowly piercing the pearly haze and striking diamond gleams from dew-drenched trees and grass as Lalia rode up to Stonewell Court which lay barely two miles east of Hildon Manor. The air was sweet with summer scents and freshened by a sea tang that brought quick colour to her cheeks.

The ride over the chalk hills proved delightful. Lalia found both Violet and Malcolm amusing and interesting companions. When they parted, Malcolm announced he had business in the village and would ride part of the way back with her.

As they set off after leaving Violet, Malcolm said, 'We are to have a guest next week, a very intelligent and interesting man who has travelled widely. My father knew him first when he was in the Embassy in Paris and Monsieur Voizard was the—'

'Monsieur Voizard?' she interrupted quickly. 'Why—I know him! I met him in London.'

'May I ask if you liked him, Mrs Brookford?'

'I found him quite charming and, as you say, very well-informed and interesting on many subjects. I should like to meet him again.'

His swift glance, followed by a faint frown, made her turn her head to hide a smile. Surely he was not jealous? And yet if he were, she knew it would please her. She was young and beautiful and used to men admiring her. Of course she was a married woman now and naturally had no intention of allowing any man to pay her unsuitable attentions; but it was pleasing to know there were men who wished to.

She was smiling as she ran up the steps of the Manor.

'So you have enjoyed your ride over the Dorset hills, I see.' Romey's voice made her look up with a start. Usually at this time he was out on the estate. 'Two angels on horseback!'

'Accompanied by a third angel—a male one,' she laughed, pulling off her stiff hat and shaking her fair curls free. 'Malcolm Overton rode with us. I like him.'

'He's an attractive young fellow and works hard.'

'He mentioned a guest whom they are expecting, a Monsieur Voizard. I met him in London when I was with Mrs Prior and her brother. Isn't it strange?'

He shot her a swift glance. 'Another admirer to trail after you?'

'What nonsense, he cannot know I am here. And what do you mean, please, by *another* admirer?'

'Young Malcolm is not often lured from his work to ride out of a morning,' he said dryly and touched her flushed cheek. 'Just remember to keep your swains at a proper distance.'

She tilted her chin. 'And what would you do if I decide to flirt with them?'

'I shall not allow you the opportunity,' he said coolly and ran down the steps to where the groom held his big raking horse, Blackie.

Lalia watched him canter down the avenue until he was hidden by a big oak that spread its gnarled branches across the driveway. He had spoken in jest of course; he could not prevent her doing anything she wished. She was free to live her own life, that had surely been part of the bargain? She bore Romey's name and wore his ring, but it was a marriage of convenience for both of them. She would not interfere with his pursuits, and he must allow her to behave as she saw fit. She went up to her room slowly, faintly disturbed by the resentment his words had aroused in her.

'I do not intend to be told how I am to behave,' she thought as she tossed her hat and riding crop onto the bed. 'If Malcolm Overton has notions of falling in love with me, he will soon get over them. And Monsieur Voizard is only an acquaintance. I know he admires me, but that is all.'

Was it all? She found herself remembering, with surprising clarity, the dark handsome Frenchman who was so often by her side, and his attractive, slightly accented voice. He had spoken mostly of music, books, and his country, but in some curious way he had made her aware of something warmer hidden beneath his conventional words. He was a clever man, versed in the ways of the world—and of women. A tiny spark of excitement lit inside her as she slipped out of her habit.

'I look forward to seeing him again,' she said aloud, 'there can be no harm in such a friendship,' and wondered uneasily why she should have said it so defiantly.

CHAPTER
EIGHT

An invitation to dine at Stonewell Court was a pleasant surprise for Lalia.

'I know you are not going into society just yet,' Mrs Overton said, 'but this is only a small family gathering, just ourselves and a friend of my husband's, Monsieur Voizard, who is staying with us.'

'We shall be delighted,' Lalia said warmly. 'I already know Monsieur Voizard.'

They were sitting in the parlour and a shaft of sunlight was making a golden halo of her hair. She made a pretty picture in her grey poplin dress brightened by the pink roses she had tucked into the bodice. Her only jewel was the emerald ring Romey had given her on their engagement, a flawless gem that had belonged to his family for generations.

'My girls are perfectly fascinated by Monsieur Voizard,' Mrs Overton remarked indulgently, 'and my husband finds his conversation delightful after so much feminine chatter.'

When the evening came, Lalia felt a flutter of excitement and happy anticipation. She had been spending her days quietly, on household matters, occasionally riding, or sitting with her mother-in-law. She still grieved for her father, but he would not, she told herself as she dressed with the aid of Minnie, her maid, have wished her to be sad and shut herself away from the world. He had loved her gay spirits and would have wanted her to laugh and enjoy life and not mourn him. And why should she mourn for Alvin who had so cruelly deceived her?

'Will you wear the diamond earrings, Ma'am?' Minnie asked eagerly as she regarded her mistress's reflection in the looking-glass, 'they'll look fine with your lovely dress.'

Lalia turned her head, watching the light fall on her piled-up curls, and decided the earrings would add a touch of brilliance. Not that she needed brilliance. Her heightened colour and the sparkle of her deeply blue eyes positively startled her for a second. *Had* she become a little weary of her peaceful existence since coming to Hildon Manor? She was young and youth demanded excitement. It was not a crime that she should feel her pulse quicken and a tiny quiver of pleasure run through her as she looked at her reflection and knew Monsieur Voizard would find her as lovely as when she had met him in London.

Romey wished her to put aside her black and grey gowns. It was impossible, of course, to wear the rose dress, but she had brought with her a white satin evening gown from which Minnie had removed the blue trimmings and substituted a silver fringe that edged the sleeves and the draped overskirt that fell into a short train at the back. A narrow black velvet ribbon, tied in a bow at the back with streamers hanging down, emphasised the dazzling whiteness of her skin. The voluminous draped skirt springing from the tight bodice accented her tiny waist and she smiled at her reflection as she rose.

'Not the French scent, Minnie, I will use eau de Cologne. Put some on my handkerchief, and bring my silver lace fan and my cloak.' She turned as someone knocked. 'See who it is, Minnie.'

It was a footman with a delicate spray of creamy rosebuds and maidenhair fern.

'The master sent 'em,' Minnie declared. 'They'll make 'ee a picture, they will, Ma'am!'

When she came into the hall, Romey's eyes widened for a second.

'A lily maid.' Something in his voice made her glance at him quickly. 'You look . . . bridal.'

'Is it unsuitable, then?' she asked anxiously. 'I know I ought to be in black or—'

'No!' He snapped the word out. 'You are done with mourning . . . unless you mourn for having been rash enough to marry me.'

She smiled as she pulled her cloak around her. 'Do you like my dress?'

'It is very beautiful,' he said and turned to the door which James held open. She followed him thoughtfully; he had not said *she* was beautiful.

The evening was a warm one, but the Overton's drawing-room was pleasantly cool. The evening scents of the garden came in the open windows, fresh and beguiling. Lalia turned from greeting her host and hostess to meet the dark eyes she remembered so well.

'I am enchanted,' Monsieur Voizard said softly as he took and held her hand. 'I had no idea I should be so lucky to meet you in Dorset. I did not know you were already married; you were engaged when we last met.'

'Oh, but I did not—' she stopped abruptly. There was no need to disclose Alvin's behaviour; let him believe it was to Romey she had been engaged.

He sensed her hesitation and said swiftly: 'I am very pleased to meet your husband. I believe his estate is not far; may I be permitted to call upon you?'

'Yes, of course. Are you still living in London, Monsieur Voizard?'

They fell into conversation and he told her that he had had an unhappy time, fearing for his parents in Paris during the siege.

'Now it is ended—and France has been humiliated.' For a moment she glimpsed the bitterness he tried to hide.

'Your country has suffered,' she murmured.

'And may suffer again if Bismarck has his wolfish way. It was a disastrous move for the Emperor to declare war to regain the support of the army . . .' he broke off. 'But these are not matters to be spoken of on an occasion such as this, forgive me.'

'I am truly sorry, Monsieur Voizard,' she let her hand rest for a second on his arm, 'you must indeed have been anxious.'

His dark eyes kindled as he met her gaze and he bowed silently.

At dinner he was placed next to her and on the other side she had Mr Overton. Malcolm sat opposite and she could not help being amused at his sulky expression. Perhaps he had hoped to sit beside her. His glances at his guest were not as friendly as they should have been and Lalia hoped Monsieur Voizard had not noticed. However he soon undeceived her.

'Young Master Malcolm has not given me quite the welcome I expected after his friendly treatment in London,' he observed, sitting back and toying with his wineglass. 'But I think I now see the reason.' He turned to smile at her. 'Do not singe the poor moth's wings too unkindly, Madame Brookford.'

She raised her fan to hide her smile. Suddenly she saw Romey looking at her. He sat beside his hostess with Violet on his right, and a faintly mocking light in his eyes made her turn quickly to talk to Mr Overton, who had much to say on the lateness of the harvest.

'Your husband is doing good work on his land,' he told her. 'He has got the right ideas and uses modern methods and cuts his losses. Once he has finished draining his land he'll be able to rent it for a good price, farmers are short of grazing land around here. And soon his sheep will begin to repay him; Dorset Horn is a good breed.'

'He intends to improve his workers' cottages,' she told him, 'and their conditions.'

'Good! Satisfied men work better and they won't be interested in this ridiculous union business.'

After dinner, when the men joined the ladies, Lalia found Monsieur Voizard at her side once again. Violet joined them and the conversation became animated.

'Monsieur Voizard declares he can beat me at the gallop,' Violet cried. 'So I have challenged him to ride with me tomorrow. Will you join us, Mrs Brookford, and be judge? I know your husband is always too busy to ride.'

Lalia agreed at once. The handsome Frenchman beside her had brought something of the elegant sophistication of his world into hers and, with it, memories of her season in London, and she listened eagerly to his amusing, sometimes faintly scandalous, accounts of society.

'Mr Morris's aesthetic movement is gaining many converts among us,' he declared. 'We are called to throw away our oil paintings and window-drapings, to dress and live more simply and naturally. This has led to a few ladies taking to living a trifle *too* naturally . . . *Tiens!* Free love is an Arcadian dream not meant for poor mortals—at least, not if they wish to be received at court.'

A little later, when Mrs Overton claimed Monsieur Voizard's attention, Violet whispered in Lalia's ear, 'You have made quite a conquest. Fanny won't forgive you, she's halfway to being in love with him! Do not forget our ride tomorrow morning.'

Romey was standing near. Later, when they were in the carriage on the way home, he said abruptly, 'What is this about riding tomorrow?'

'Oh, it is some prank of Violet's. She thinks she can out-gallop Monsieur and has bid me come and be judge.'

'A silly prank. You had better forget it, Lalia.'

She turned to look at him, but the darkness hid his face.

'But I have promised to go, Romey. It will look rude if I don't.'

'It will look strange if you do,' he spoke shortly. 'People must have noticed how he singled you out for his attentions tonight.'

'If you mean the Overtons, I am perfectly certain they saw nothing but natural good manners on his part,' she returned. 'You forget I knew him in London.'

'I would rather you did not ride tomorrow.'

She was swept with a sudden anger. 'Romey, it was agreed we were both free in our marriage. You speak as if you do not trust me—and I do not like it! Monsieur Voizard may admire me, and show it; he is a man who probably admires many women. French men are not so rigid in their manner towards women, they are naturally gallant and it means nothing.'

'I do not wish you to go.'

She sank back in her corner and found she was trembling. What right had he to forbid a harmless ride with Violet and the Frenchman? She and Romey had agreed that each of them should go their own way and it was most unfair of him to spoil her enjoyment of an innocent morning's amusement! She was silent for the rest of the drive and went to her room after a brief 'Goodnight' in the hall. It was the first time they had seriously disagreed and she felt a trifle uneasy, but was determined to show him she was not to be bullied.

'If I give in now,' she thought as Minnie unpinned her hair and began to brush it, 'I shall be in a weaker position next time.'

Romey had left the house by the time she came downstairs next morning. She sent a message to the stables to bring her little mare to the door, but was told that by Romey's order the mare had been sent to the

village with a groom on some errand. She bit her lip as her
anger awoke.

She said: 'Tell Simpson I wish to see him.'

When the groom came, cap in hand, she said: 'Since my
mare is out, I shall ride Blackie. Saddle him for me
please.'

'Eh, but Blackie's the Master's horse, Ma'am,' Simpson's weather-beaten face looked startled. 'He'm no
horse for a lady. Blackie's a bad-tempered critter, all vuss
and vidget.'

'I know how to handle a bad-tempered horse. Bring
him around at once, Simpson.'

Simpson looked unhappy. 'Don't know what Master'll
zay . . .'

'That will be quite all right.'

She thrust her untasted coffee aside, too angry to drink
it. How dare Romey take her mare from her! If he thought
to force her to obey his ridiculous and unreasonable
demands, she would have to teach him she had a will of
her own.

At first sight of Blackie rolling his eyes and restlessly
pawing the gravel, she had a twinge of uncertainty. He did
look very big and rather too spirited. But she was a good
rider and knew how to manage her horse. Simpson, his
uneasiness apparent on his ruddy face, helped her to
mount.

'Ma'am, you'll mind his ways and not cross him if he
shows a mite of temper?' he begged. 'I don't like the
thought on't; I'm fair worrit. 'Tis not safe for a lady to ride
him . . .'

'Don't worry, Simpson,' she smiled down at his anxious
face, 'I shall not be out for long and Blackie can rid himself
of his temper by a gallop over the hills.'

She was relieved to find the horse behaving peaceably.
She could feel the muscles that moved smoothly under
her and her arms felt the pull when he wished to return to

the stables at first. But he showed no signs of misbehaving and she grew confident as triumph filled her and she thought how she had out-witted Romey!

Violet and Monsieur Voizard were waiting for her. As the Frenchman's dark eyes met hers she felt a tiny prickle of excitement and a quickening of pulse before she looked away.

'A very beautiful lady on a beautiful horse,' he murmured as he rode close to her, 'but he looks a little too big and strong for you.'

'Oh!' Violet noticed Blackie for the first time. 'Are you allowed to ride Blackie? Your husband usually rides him and says he has a hard mouth. Should you be riding him, dear Mrs Brookford?'

'Of course. He is behaving beautifully. Let us make for Cleve Hill and you can have your race.'

There was little chance of meeting Romey on the ride and he would still be out when she returned, but Lalia thought it might not be wise to linger too long on the grassy chalk hills. There was really no need for him to know anything; Simpson, if she asked him, would be silent on the matter. She was uncomfortably aware of a change in her attitude. She had left Hildon Manor determined Romey should know she had defied him and had not been prevented from riding, but as her anger cooled she experienced a slight feeling of guilt and she knew that, annoyed as Romey would be at her riding with Voizard, he would be much angrier to know she had ridden Blackie!

'You are looking *un peu triste*, Madame Brookford,' Monsieur Voizard's voice brought her out of her thoughts and she turned to smile at him.

'Oh no, I'm always happy when I can ride. It is so lovely here, the sea is like a bowl of diamonds this morning. Let us ride on.'

They cantered briskly towards the sea. Blackie showed

an inclination to pull ahead, as if he wished to lead the others, and Lalia had trouble in restraining him. Suddenly Violet cried,

'There, along that stretch of grass, as far as that bank. I'll race you, Monsieur Voizard! Mrs Brookford, pray hold Blackie in well or he may try to join us.'

With a flourish of whips they were off, Violet's veil flying out behind her. It was obvious the Frenchman was the better rider, but he did not press his horse and Lalia guessed he intended Violet to win. Suddenly she felt Blackie's muscles quiver; he backed restlessly, snorted and reared so abruptly she nearly lost her seat. She dragged on the reins but Blackie paid no heed. He would not stay still while a race was on! He rushed forward and with a gasp of dismay Lalia realised she could not hold him in and it was all she could do to stay in the saddle! The thunder of hoofs behind them made the others turn and Violet cried out something Lalia did not catch. Then Monsieur Voizard was racing beside her, shouting,

'Try to turn him . . . Do not let him take the bank—there is a lane . . .'

It was too late! She felt the horse bunch his great muscles as he rose in a leap that cleared the bank. As he crashed against the far bank of the hidden lane she felt herself slipping . . . sliding . . . then blackness!

CHAPTER
NINE

A GREY mist . . . pain . . . Violet's voice saying: 'She's coming round. Oh, Monsieur Voizard, is she badly hurt?'

'I do not think so, that bush broke her fall.'

'She should not have been allowed to ride that wicked horse! What can Mr Brookford have been thinking of to let her? Will you ride for help, Monsieur Voizard? I shall stay with her.'

Lalia opened her eyes to see Violet's anxious face bending over her. The mist was clearing and the pain had resolved itself into an ache from many bruises. She whispered, 'Romey did not know I took Blackie out . . . Is the horse injured?'

'His legs are cut, but he has galloped home most joyfully,' the Frenchman told her grimly, 'after having done his best to kill you. I shall ride to Hildon Manor and—'

'Look, someone is coming,' Violet stood up, shading her eyes with her hand. 'They knew there had been an accident when Blackie came back alone.'

'Your husband comes,' Monsieur Voizard said. 'No, do not rise . . .'

'I—I am not hurt,' Lalia struggled up, wincing as pain caught her, 'just bruised. Help me to stand, Violet.'

'Pray lie still,' Violet begged, but Lalia got to her feet with the help of Monsieur Voizard and stood, swaying a little as the group of horsemen rode up.

Romey swung himself off his horse and strode over. 'How did it happen? Are you hurt, Lalia? Can you manage to ride back or shall I send the men for a cart?'

Avoiding his eyes, she said: 'I am only bruised, I can ride; there are no bones broken.'

'I was not happy when I saw she had chosen that horse,' Violet said, 'he is not a lady's horse.'

'But perhaps there was no other horse for Madame to ride this morning,' Monsieur Voizard said gently and Lalia, looking at him quickly, saw his eyes resting on Romey. 'She is indeed lucky to escape so well. If I can be of any help—'

'Thank you, no,' Romey's voice was curt. 'Come, Lalia, see if you can manage to mount.'

The ride back was slow and painful for Lalia. She gritted her teeth, forcing herself to fight off the feeling of faintness as her bruised body protested at the movement. Romey rode close beside her, holding her horse's rein and the two grooms and Simpson rode behind. When they reached the house, Romey swung her down and carried her up the steps where Mrs Grant was anxiously waiting.

'Oh deary me! Is the poor child badly hurt, sir?' the housekeeper came forward quickly.

'Only bruised, I think, but I'll send for Doctor Green to make sure. Is her bed ready?'

'Yes, sir.'

Lalia was undressed by Mrs Grant and Minnie and put to bed. She lay watching them moving about the room, putting away her clothes; Minnie took the muddied riding habit off to be dried and brushed. Her thoughts spun round in uneasy circles. She knew Romey was angry, very angry. She had behaved recklessly, determined to have her own way as she had always had it. Admittedly it had been a mistake to take Blackie out, but it would never have happened if Romey had not behaved in such a high-handed manner. It was all his fault and he had no right to be angry with her! But he *was* angry, she had seen it in the grim set of his chin and mouth and the steely glint in his eyes.

Doctor Green found no broken bones, but a painful multiplicity of bruises, and advised a light diet and several days in bed.

'There is often something of shock in such cases,' she heard him say to Romey outside her door, 'you will do well to keep her quiet for some days.'

Mrs Brookford came to sit by her bed and her gentle presence was welcome. Lalia knew she was suffering pain as she watched the pale, patient face and she waited until Minnie had done tidying the room and had left, before saying,

'Dear Mother Edith, will you consent to my taking you to London to consult this Austrian doctor whose treatment of rheumatic conditions has been so successful? Monsieur Voizard has spoken to me of Doctor Helmer for whom he has most high praise.'

'Oh, my dear child, I have long accepted I shall never be cured. I assure you I am quite better sometimes. You must not be anxious for me.'

'But it would be worth a trial,' Lalia urged. As she eased her aching body into a more comfortable position she wondered what it must be like never to be free of pain. She would speak to Romey about it . . . but Romey was still angry with her. He had come to stand by her bed, looking down at her, his face devoid of expression. He had asked her how she was feeling, ordered Minnie to lower the blind to keep the direct light out of her eyes, told her he was sending her a glass of claret and she was to drink it, and left her. No doubt he was waiting until she was recovered enough to bear his reproof.

As her weakness left her, her resentment returned, although she could no longer pretend it was all Romey's fault. She *had* been unwise, but she was not at all sure she was going to admit it.

The warm weather was drifting imperceptibly into autumn. The mornings were veiled in faint blue mists and trees had an overblown look. Blackberries were ripening in hedgerows and sea winds, when they came, had an edge to them.

Romey had had to go to London on business to do with repairs to the house and Lalia, recovered but still a trifle stiff, watched his return with mixed emotions from the parlour window. She heard his quick step in the hall and his voice giving orders to James and felt her heart jolt dismayingly as the door opened and he came in.

'How do you feel now?' He crossed the room with swift strides and took both her hands in his. 'Are your bruises healed? You still look too pale for my liking.'

She said, a little breathlessly: 'I am perfectly recovered, thank you. Did you have a pleasant visit to London?'

He grimaced. 'I have no love for cities. However, I got my business done, and work here can begin in a few weeks. It must be done before winter sets in. How is my mother these days?'

'Not very well, I fear. Romey, I want to take her to London to try Doctor Helmer's treatment, so many people speak well of him. Will you persuade her to go?'

He nodded. 'I shall, and it had better be soon. It will be as well if you are both out of the house when work begins. I'll go to mother now and tell her.' He walked to the door.

'Romey,' Lalia spoke swiftly before her courage failed her, 'aren't you going to say anything about my taking Blackie out that morning? I realise I should not have done it, but . . .'

He turned, his hand on the door handle, and looked at her hard while she waited, uneasy at the touch of panic that caught her.

'It was a stupid, rather childish thing to have done,' he

said deliberately. 'The charming Monsieur Voizard makes his admiration of you too obvious for my liking. Perhaps you think you can control such admiration—as you thought you could control Blackie.'

Her eyes widened suddenly. 'Romey—you aren't *jealous*, are you?'

His short laugh dispelled the idea. 'No, Lalia, not jealous of you, rest assured. But I am jealous of the good name of my wife. We made a bargain, but it implied you would respect your position as my wife.'

'But of course I will. You mistake Monsieur's manner. I—I realise I ought not to have ridden Blackie,' she raised her chin defiantly, 'but it was your fault for not letting me have my mare.'

'Yes,' he agreed unexpectedly, 'I should have known you would try to outwit me. You have been punished enough for what you did. Let us forget the matter.'

He smiled a little mockingly and left her to wonder if she would ever understand him. She had expected him to be furious and to scold her, and he had dismissed her burst of self-assertion as a childish act!

The next day Mrs Brookford told her Romey had persuaded her to go to London.

'He wishes us to go at once,' she sighed. 'I'm sure I do not look forward to such an upheaval and having to burden you with looking after me.'

Lalia assured her she was delighted at her decision and they fell to making plans for the journey.

Romey contacted agents and found them apartments in Curzon Street. They were to take Mrs Grant and Minnie with them, and a young groom to drive the landau to be hired for their stay. Lalia had written for an appointment with Doctor Helmer, and all was set for their departure under Romey's care in two weeks' time.

Romey saw them installed in the pleasant rooms he had rented in London. He called upon Doctor Helmer and appeared satisfied with the visit. When he said goodbye, he held Lalia's hand, looking down at her.

'I know you will look after my mother. You have been kind, Lalia, in thinking so much of her welfare. Do you find it a change from thinking so much of yourself?'

She gasped and tried to withdraw her hand, but his grasp tightened upon it.

'That is a horribly unkind thing to say!'

'Probably; the truth is often unkind. I told you that you had been spoiled all your life by your father and aunt; it is not entirely your fault that you are—'

'Vain, selfish—and cruel!' she flashed at him, her eyes bright with indignation.

His sudden laugh infuriated her. 'Do not despair too much, my dear wife, I begin to see an improvement.' He bent forward and kissed her lightly on her cheek. 'Behave yourself, if you don't, I shall take you back to Hildon Manor.'

She stood for a moment, staring into space, after he had left her. Her cheek tingled where his lips had touched it. Only once before, on her wedding day, had he kissed her. She turned slowly and went to help Mrs Grant arrange Mrs Brookford's bedroom.

Two days later, Doctor Helmer examined Mrs Brookford and held out hope, if not for a complete cure, at least for a less painful condition.

'I feel it is too good to be true,' Mrs Brookford sighed when they returned.

'I believe it *is* true,' Lalia declared joyfully. 'Now you must have your rest, it has been a tiring morning for you.'

She was writing to Romey to let him know how his mother's first visit to the doctor had gone, when Mrs Grant entered, looking a trifle flustered, and announced: 'Mr Voizard.'

Lalia swung around and, as she met his dark eyes, her heart missed a beat. She sprang up and came to meet him.

'Monsieur Voizard! I did not know you had returned to London.'

'Did you think I would remain in Dorset when you are here?' His gaze seemed to burn her and for a second she was uneasy, then the pleasure of seeing him thrust all else from her mind.

'I am pleased to see you,' she said sedately. 'My mother-in-law is to undergo treatment with Doctor Helmer here.'

'So Mrs Overton tells me.' He spoke quickly as if he, too, felt unexpected emotion. 'Mrs Brookford, will you allow me to visit you? May I show you something of London? Your mother-in-law will not need all your time, surely?'

'Oh *no*! I am still in mourning . . . and it would not be proper, you must see that. But if you wish to visit Mrs Brookford and myself, we shall be pleased to see you.'

He bowed, but not before she had seen the faint smile hovering around his lips.

'I shall be grateful for small mercies, most lovely and enchanting lady—and live in hope,' he murmured.

CHAPTER
TEN

MRS BROOKFORD had treatment three times a week at the
clinic. Nervous at first, she soon began to look forward to
her visits and the relief they were slowly bringing her and
her spirits brightened as the days passed.

During the time her mother-in-law rested, Lalia went
shopping, visited museums and exhibitions and drove in
the park in the carriage Romey had hired for her. The
vivid tints of the trees and displays of autumn flowers, the
cheerful crowds, and children with their nurses amused
and interested her. She made no effort to contact any of
her relations; they had shown no interest in her and she
had no intention of thrusting herself upon them.

Monsieur Voizard called often, always when Mrs
Brookford was present. His manner was all it should be,
but Lalia suspected he was biding his time and found
excitement in the knowledge that he could not keep away
from her. She faced the fact that he was more dangerous
than she had realised. His charm, when he chose to exert
it, was very potent and he knew how to please a woman, to
make her feel beautiful, enchanting, desired. His flattery
was too subtle to resent, his sophistication a challenge.
He was different from any man she had known and
more exciting in the very danger he represented.

He stopped her carriage in the park one morning to
speak to her.

'Is it possible you would honour me by joining a small
party at the house of a friend of mine?' he asked, his eyes
appreciative of her lavender dress and ribbon-trimmed

bonnet. 'My friend is an artist and this is to display some of his work which he will be putting in an exhibition soon.'

'Oh no, Monsieur Voizard. It is most kind of you, but I could not do so.' He did not miss the faint regret in her voice.

'It is a very innocent occasion, dear Madame—and there will be only a few people and no one who knows you. My friend plans to serve a little supper, he has a fine taste in wine. And his paintings are interesting.'

'It sounds delightful, but no, I am afraid it is impossible. My mother-in-law would be quite shocked, I think.' Lalia sighed, thinking of the long evenings after Mrs Brookford had retired to bed.

'Need she know?' The question startled her and she stared at him, frowning slightly. He went on coolly: 'You could say you visited an old friend, there would be no harm in so small a lie. To be in London, so exciting a city with so much to offer . . . It is wrong for you to be hidden away! You are beautiful, young, full of life and fire! Madame, I implore you, think about it . . . and let me know what you decide.'

She shook her head and bade him good morning. But as she was driven away, she knew his words would stay with her, teasing her, tempting her . . .

What harm could come of such an innocuous gathering? She knew something of art and always visited galleries when in London. It would be interesting to have a private view of an artist's work and perhaps meet some of his artist friends. No one would ever know.

'And if they *did* come to know,' she thought rebelliously, 'what harm? I am not doing anything shocking like meeting Claude Voizard alone, or going to a theatre with him. But I wouldn't like to deceive dear Mother Edith.'

She was sitting with Mrs Brookford that evening when, on a sudden impulse, she said casually, 'I have had an invitation to spend an evening viewing some paintings which are to be exhibited later, but of course I probably should not go.'

Mrs Brookford looked up from her embroidery. 'I do not see why, my dear. It is not like going to a ball or theatre or a big social affair. It is dull for you I fear, sitting alone in the evenings.'

Lalia waited for her to ask the name of her friend who had given the invitation, but Mrs Brookford said no more, evidently assuming it was some relation or woman friend. Lalia's pulse quickened; she could accept Claude Voizard's invitation, her mother-in-law had not forbidden it.

'And it is possible she would not object if she knew it was he,' she thought. 'She likes him and considers him a perfect gentleman.'

Romey, if he knew, would certainly not give his permission. But Romey did not know they had met Monsieur Voizard. Mrs Brookford suffered pain in her hands and could not write easily and Lalia wrote her letters for her, and when Mrs Brookford mentioned Monsieur's having called and sent flowers and fruit, Lalia had left it out and Mrs Brookford had not noticed the omission.

Her note accepting the invitation was answered by a sheaf of roses, but no card accompanied it, which intrigued her. Perhaps it was part of his charm that she never felt perfectly certain of him. But when he called next morning and they were alone for a moment, he murmured he would send his carriage for her at nine o'clock.

'So late?' she demurred.

'That is early for Londoners.'

'I must not be late back.'

'But of course not, you shall leave when you wish.'

Since going into half-mourning she had ordered an

amethyst satin evening gown which she decided to wear. It heightened her delicate colouring and she knew she was looking her best when she stepped from the carriage to meet Monsieur Voizard.

He slid his hand inside her cloak, touching her bare arm.

'You are an enchantress! Your beauty is a magic no man can resist. My friend will want to paint you.'

She laughed, pretending not to notice the pressure on her arm or the tiny thrill it sent through her. For a second she was uneasy; had she been rash? Could she trust herself with this dangerously attractive man? She pushed the thought aside and let him lead her into a small house and up a flight of stairs to a room where unframed paintings crowded the walls.

Monsieur Roche, the artist, bowed over her hand and murmured greetings. There were about fifteen people in the room. The men were in informal dress and several of the women had adopted the new 'aesthetic' style and were draped in sage green garments and had Greek-type coiffures.

A buffet supper was served. Claude Voizard, always by her side, introduced her to people and persuaded her to drink some of his friend's 'fine wine'. The paintings interested her as did the comments of the other guests, most of whom were artists or people who wrote about art. She found it all delightful, the soft lighting, the murmur of voices and the admiration in the men's eyes. Excitement mounted to her head, like the wine. After her quiet country life in Dorset and dull evenings in the apartment, she felt liberated, alive, glowing!

Suddenly she realised the time.

'I must be going, I had no idea it was so late!' She caught up her train hastily.

'I shall take you back,' he said, 'it is not so very late.'

The night was cool and crisp and stars blazed from an indigo sky.

'Have you enjoyed the evening?' Claude Voizard asked softly.

'It was delightful. I think Monsieur Roche has true talent, I admired his work.'

'And I admire *you*—more than any woman I know! Lalia, I must talk to you! We are at your apartment, let me come in for a minute, only one minute, I implore you!'

'Oh no! It is quite impossible!'

'You are afraid? You do not trust me—or perhaps yourself? I had not thought you a coward, Lalia.'

She hesitated, the very danger of the situation making her reckless.

'Very well—but it must be only for a minute.'

He followed her into the little room downstairs used for meals. As she turned to him, he caught her in his arms and held her in a frightening clasp. She could feel him trembling as his mouth closed on hers. She was unable to free herself! His kisses were making her faint and she ceased to struggle! She was drowning in a whirlpool of emotion . . .

Suddenly she wrenched herself free. '*No* . . .'

'My angel! I love you, you must know it! And you—'

'You must go,' she whispered, shrinking back.

'Yes, it is certainly time Monsieur Voizard left,' a voice said behind them.

Lalia choked back a cry of dismay as Romey stepped out from the shadowed doorway.

Late autumn gales had stripped much of the foliage from the trees and what was left had taken on a dull brownish tinge. In the gardens, a few apples clung to leafless branches while Michaelmas daisies, asters and dahlias strove bravely to brighten the untidy flowerbeds. Occasionally a sumach blazed in rose and gold, standing out from the dun-coloured background. Fitful sunshine reflected from ponds and streams, and the pools collected in cart-tracks on country lanes.

From the window of the railway carriage, Lalia watched the country scene sweeping past. In spite of her fur jacket, she felt cold. A porter had placed a footwarmer at her feet by Romey's order, but the chill that gripped her came from within. Except for the steady clack-clack of the train wheels and occasional rustle of Romey's newspaper, all was silent in the compartment.

The shock of seeing Romey was still with her. Claude Voizard had recovered himself with practised assurance, mentioning having escorted Madame Brookford home from attending an exhibition of paintings, and had left with an ease she envied. No such ease helped her when Romey turned to look at her and she saw the steely anger in his eyes.

When, stammering and hot-cheeked, she expressed her surprise at not being notified of his arrival, he told her curtly his decision had been unplanned. She had waited, her heart thudding, for his anger to burst forth, but he had merely said: 'You had better go to bed. See that your cases are packed, we are returning to Dorset tomorrow.'

'To Dorset? But I cannot leave your mother—'

'Mrs Grant and Minnie are perfectly capable of looking after her.'

'I do not wish to return,' she said, locking her fingers together so he should not see how they trembled.

'I am aware of that,' his mouth tightened for a moment, 'nevertheless, you will come with me tomorrow.'

'And if I refuse?'

'You won't. You will come home before your reputation is tarnished.'

'How dare you! I have done nothing to warrant your saying such a thing!'

'I don't suppose you have. But you are well on the way

to making a fool of yourself over Voizard, and I shall not allow it. I shall be here for you at nine o'clock tomorrow morning.' He turned on his heel and left the room.

Mrs Brookford had accepted the explanation that Romey wanted his wife at Hildon Manor to advise on some of the work being done there and said she was quite happy to have Mrs Grant looking after her. When Romey came next morning he greeted his mother before seeing Lalia's cases loaded into the cab and driving off with her to the station. He did not speak to her or glance at her and his face had the shuttered look she had seen once before.

'I have had to return because I could not quarrel and defy him before his mother,' she thought bitterly, 'she would have been greatly distressed and it would have been bad for her health. But I shall not allow myself to be bullied in this manner! When we get home I shall make it plain I intend to lead my own life.'

The carriage was at Dorchester to meet them. Lalia lay back against the cushions, her thoughts fixed on the coming scene with Romey as they drove through the town and into the country and at last to Hildon Manor where workmen were already busy on the roof.

Romey broke the silence as they went into the house.

'Rain has been coming in upstairs, the repairs to the slates are just in time. Tea will be ready for you in the parlour when you have taken off your wraps.'

'And *I* shall be ready to make my position clear,' she told herself as the resentment simmering inside her threatened to burst into a blaze of anger.

When she entered the parlour he was standing before the fireplace where a bright log fire blazed. A tray on the table before the fire held tea things, hot scones and cake. She seated herself before it and began to pour out tea, feeling a need of something to drive out her chill. Suddenly she was unable to stay silent any longer. Putting down her cup she said, lifting her chin as she stared at him,

'It is time we came to an understanding, Romey. Our marriage is not as other marriages, it was a bargain struck between us, you have my fortune to use and I accepted your name and protection and was free to live as I wished. I think it was a fair bargain.'

'Perfectly fair; in fact I got the bigger share and I am aware of it. But you are my wife and that position does not allow you to misbehave.'

'I have *never* misbehaved!' she cried, her cheeks flaming. 'Because I chose to go to a private viewing with Monsieur Voizard, is *that* misbehaving?'

'Since he is in love with you, and you are on the brink of becoming infatuated with him—yes, it does.'

She sprang to her feet, all caution cast away.

'You should have married a nonentity! A pretty little doll without will or mind of her own! Why did you not marry one of the Grange girls? They would have hastened to obey your lightest command. But I forget . . . neither of them had a fortune, and you wanted a Golden Bride, didn't you?'

He took a quick step towards her, then stopped. The door had opened and James, his face a blank, announced, 'Lady Darrencourt.'

Lalia swung around with a gasp. The small figure wrapped in a paisley shawl walked over to the fire and held both hands out to it.

'So you see,' Rosa looked over her shoulder, smiling, 'I have come back.'

CHAPTER
ELEVEN

WORDS deserted Lalia; sheer shock held her motionless as she stared unbelievingly at the woman who had caused her so much pain and humiliation. The faint bravado beneath Rosa's words had not escaped her notice; so Rosa had come to flaunt herself before her! The woman for whom Alvin had thrown away honour and loyalty.

Romey was the first to speak. 'You are chilled. Put your feet on the fender, it will warm them.' He turned to Lalia. 'Give her some tea.'

When Lalia did not move, he poured out the tea and took it, with the plate of scones, to the figure crouching over the fire.

'Ah!' Rosa snatched at the plate. 'I did not have the time to get food on the journey.' She ate the scones eagerly and drank the tea and gave her cup to be refilled.

Lalia found her voice. 'What do you mean by coming here? How did you know where to find me?'

'It was easy. Alvin's mother sometimes writes to him. Oh, such unpleasant letters saying quite horrid things about me. She told him you had married Romey and come to Dorset.' She let her shawl slip from her shoulders. 'It was very wrong of you to let strangers have Winterbridge Hall, it is my home.'

'No! It is no longer your home!' Lalia's voice shook with suppressed fury and she ignored the quick glance Romey sent her. 'You have disgraced us! You chose your life, go back to it!'

Rosa tossed her head. 'You forget I am still Lady Darrencourt.'

'You did not marry Alvin?' Romey's voice cut in.

'No,' she looked away. 'Of course, he begged me to, but I refused. I was tired of Jamaica so I came back. Winterbridge is mine, and the money too. Sir Ashley made provisions for me in his will.'

'A will which he revoked when you disgraced him,' Lalia told her fiercely. 'You get *nothing*! After the way you behaved you stand little chance if you try to contest the will.' She picked up the shawl and flung it around Rosa's shoulders. 'You are a wicked, cruel woman! I never wish to see you again. Leave this house this instant!'

Rosa had risen, gripping her shawl with hands that trembled. For the first time Lalia noticed how pale she was and how hollow her cheeks had become, but it only added fuel to her anger and disgust.

'Leave this house, I tell you!'

Rosa glanced furtively at Romey, then her eyes came back to Lalia standing stiffly before her, her lovely face implacable.

'I . . . have nowhere to go,' she whispered.

'Sit down,' Romey said abruptly. 'Tell me, why didn't you go to your mother in Spain?'

'I—I never told her,' Rosa's voice faltered. 'She thinks I have been with Sir Ashley in Jamaica. She is—is very strict and I feared . . . She is poor and she cannot help me. And there are my sisters, it will spoil their chances of a good marriage if—if—'

'If their disgraced sister were to arrive on their doorstep,' Lalia cried scornfully. 'You must return to Jamaica—and your lover.'

'Why cannot you return to Jamaica?' Romey asked quietly.

Rosa looked from one to another. The tip of her tongue

flicked out, moistening her dry lips as she hesitated. A
painful flush suffused her face and she said unsteadily,
'Alvin has—has thrown me over. He . . . is tired of me.
He has not treated me well and I have been very unhappy!
He has other women, half-breed women. He paid my
passage home but has given me no money, *nothing*. And
his family hate me and will never help me.'

Silence fell in which Lalia could hear Rosa's quick
uneven breathing. She found she was unable to look away
from the small figure by the fire, even though it was
hateful to her. Suddenly she burst out.

'I will not have you here! You were the cause of my
father's death! You killed him! When you eloped, he had
a stroke and never recovered. You are a—'

'Stop!' Romey ordered her sternly, 'she is going to
faint.' He moved in time to catch Rosa as she slipped to
the floor. 'Ring for a maid. She is shivering; she may be
ill.'

Lalia hesitated, then pulled the bell. When the footman came she sent for a housemaid.

'She cannot stay here, Romey, I will not let her.'

'I'm afraid you will have to. You can't turn a sick
woman out. How did she arrive?'

'In farmer Smith's cart, sir,' the maid who was chafing
Rosa's hands said. 'I saw it set her down at the bend in the
avenue.'

'Get a room ready—and heat the bed. And get
some hot broth.' He turned to Lalia. 'I think she's half-
starved, she's as light as a feather. She must stay the
night.'

'Very well.' Lalia set her lips sternly and turned away.
Much as she hated Rosa, she could not turn her out on a
cold autumn evening if she were a sick woman. 'I will see
to it.'

She left Rosa in the care of the maids who undressed
her and put her to bed and brought her beef broth and

bread. Later, one of the maids who had some knowledge of nursing told Lalia she thought Rosa was suffering mostly from exhaustion and lack of food.

'She's as thin as a sparrow, Ma'am. She's taken her supper and she's sleeping. Lizzie and I will keep our eyes on her, but 'tis my opinion she'll sleep through the night and maybe most of the morning.'

'Thank you. If she is restless, give her a cordial.' Lalia turned away. What did the staff make of this sudden appearance of the disgraced woman, the adultress who had been the cause of Sir Ashley's death? She put her hand to her burning forehead, feeling sick and knowing it was the aftermath of shock.

At dinner, Romey said abruptly: 'You're eating nothing.'

'I am not hungry.'

'All the same, you must eat something.' He signalled to the footman to bring back the dish of chicken mousse and rather than have an argument, she took some and forced herself to eat, and to drink a glass of wine.

When the drawing-room door shut behind the footman who had brought the coffee, Romey dropped the curtain he had raised to look out of the window.

'I think there may be a frost tonight, the sky is clear and the stars bright.' He came over to Lalia and sat down beside her on the sofa. 'This has been a great shock to you, I know. Are you feeling all right? You are pale. You have every right to be angry, to despise and distrust Rosa after her behaviour. I know what you are feeling, Lalia, and I am deeply sorry that this has happened.' His voice was gentle and his eyes no longer cold. 'Neither of us wants her here. She is a trouble-maker and she has forfeited all right to our help or forgiveness.'

'I shall *never* forgive her!'

'I do not expect you to, your hurt has been too deep. But we cannot throw her out, she has no money, nowhere to go, no hope of help from anyone.'

'And whose fault is that, pray?' Lalia demanded, her eyes flashing.

'Her own. But would you drive her out, knowing how she is situated?'

'I—I shall let her stay until she is stronger, then she must go. Alvin must look after her.'

'Alvin will do nothing,' Romey said grimly. 'I haven't told you, but I heard from a man who does business with Jamaica that Alvin is going to pieces. Drink, women and gambling are ruining him. The estate is a large and valuable one, but if he neglects it and wastes the income from it . . .' He shrugged. 'Alvin always had a weak streak. His treatment of Rosa is not a complete surprise to me; I know him pretty well.'

Lalia was silent. She felt bruised and shaken after her outburst of anger. Weariness stole over her as she leaned back against the cushions with the firelight playing on her crown of fair curls. How was she going to endure the presence of Rosa in her home?

A sudden twist in her thoughts made her glance at Romey from under her long lashes. He had said no more, and she had thought no more, of the quarrel that had been brewing before Rosa entered the room. Would he return to it and would she have to do battle with him? She was too tired, too exhausted emotionally to withstand it. She said wearily,

'Please do not let us quarrel about Claude Voizard, Romey. You are right, I *was* attracted by him and perhaps I was slightly infatuated, as you said. But I did nothing wrong . . .' Her colour deepened as she thought of the strange and disturbing sensations that had swept her while in the Frenchman's arms. Was it possible she might have done wrong if Romey had not come? She flinched from the thought. 'Please—can we forget it?'

'I have already done so. You are not the first woman to

find him irresistible. I have you safe at home.' He got up and stood with his broad shoulders resting against the mantelpiece. 'I'm going to send you to bed, you're drooping like a tired child. Come,' he held out his hand and she allowed him to raise her to her feet. He slipped his arm around her waist and went with her to the door. 'I'll tell Mrs Grant to give you some hot milk and honey, it will help you to sleep.'

For a moment she leant against him, finding a strange comfort in his nearness and his firm arm around her.

'Thank you, you are kind to me.' She raised her eyes to his. 'I am glad we have not quarrelled; we're friends, aren't we?'

Something in his face startled her, then it was gone and he said, 'Friends, yes. That is what you wish, isn't it, Lalia?'

'Of course. It is what you wish too, isn't it?'

He did not answer. Instead, he bent his dark head and kissed her lightly on her forehead.

'Sleep well. Tomorrow we shall consider the situation with Rosa.'

To her surprise she did sleep well. When she awoke, the maid told her Rosa was still sleeping. She dressed and went down to find Romey finishing his breakfast. He rose at her entrance and she thought he looked strained and as if he had not slept well. Perhaps he had been more disturbed by Rosa's arrival than she had thought.

'I am to make an inspection of some cottages this morning,' he told her.

'Can I come with you?' she asked at once.

He agreed and when she was ready they set off in the dogcart he liked to drive. As he had predicted, there had been a frost during the night and now the fields and woods were dewy and sparkling and patches of rapidly melting frost glimmered palely in corners where the sun's rays had not yet explored. The air was still and exhilaratingly fresh and the sky stretched above them, a fathomless sapphire dome. The horses were fresh and mettlesome and in spite of yesterday's upset, Lalia, wrapped cosily in her furs with her curls escaping from under her velvet bonnet, felt her spirits rise as she listened to Romey's description of the improvements he planned.

The men were at work, but their wives, with children peering curiously from behind their skirts, curtseyed and looked at Lalia's furs and glowing face with wide eyes.

She was horrified with what she saw. A single room, with an earthen floor, divided into two, in which a man and six children crowded; the walls stained with smoke, the tiny windows and fetid air made her suddenly ashamed of the warmth and comfort of her home. The children were barefoot, and in one hovel a wizened baby lay whining miserably while the mother, a grey-faced woman aged before her time, fed two small children with gruel.

'Oh Romey, we *must* do something!' she exclaimed when at last they turned to drive back. 'It shocks me to see how they live.'

'We shall do something and as soon as possible,' he assured her. 'The men will soon be earning more money and the cottages and land around them will be drained so the people can make a garden and keep hens and perhaps a goat. I shall give them the animals and the children can have the milk. Times have been bad for agricultural workers. Our present government is too preoccupied with France's war with Prussia to take heed of what is necessary in this country.'

'This compulsory education act of parliament will help the children read and write, but it will not give them shoes or fill their empty stomachs,' Lalia said bitterly. She looked up suddenly and caught his eyes upon her and a flash of insight told her what he was thinking. 'Yes, I *can* think of others than myself,' she said defensively. 'You do not believe it, I know.'

'But I do believe it, now. Admit it, Lalia, when you lived in Winterbridge Hall you had your own way in everything. You had too much freedom for your years and too much admiration from your admirers and far too great an idea of the importance of the beautiful Miss Lalia Darrencourt.'

She gasped, the shock of his words was like a cold douche.

'You are . . . are . . .'

'A remarkably truthful man,' he supplied tranquilly, 'who is often driven to speak his mind. Now you are furious with me.'

'Of course I am! No—I'm not. I don't believe you mean all of it. I *ought* to be furious.' She looked away, thinking that he was right, she *had* believed she was someone special for whom everything must be comfortable and happy. She thought of something: 'You made no mention of my being *cruel* this time.'

'I'm waiting to see if you are.' His reply surprised her and she looked at him quickly, but his face told her nothing.

When she reached the house she shed her furs and went reluctantly to Rosa's room.

Rosa was sitting up in bed in one of Lalia's nainsook nightgowns and a lacy little jacket, also Lalia's. She had a little more colour in her cheeks and her eyes, though wary, were brighter as she greeted Lalia.

'Indeed I have slept wonderfully,' she said in answer to Lalia's enquiry. 'It is a charming room, and so warm. It was dreadfully cold on the steamer, I did not have at all a pleasant voyage. But I was glad to leave Jamaica. You had better know that Alvin is drinking himself into his grave.' She pushed back a lock of silky hair. 'He began shortly after we arrived and would not heed my warnings.

It is as well you did not marry him, Lalia.'

'Did you have any true love for him?' Lalia demanded.

Rosa looked down and for a second her mouth trembled.

'I did fall in love with him, and he said he loved me and could not live without me. He begged and *begged* me to run away with him. And you know, Sir Ashley was very kind and I liked him, but he *was* too old for me. Oh, I know I did a great wrong, but Alvin . . . Truly I could not resist him.'

Lalia was silent. Against her will came memories of her own unhappy suspicions that her father had made a tragic mistake and such a marriage must end in disaster. Rosa had hot Spanish blood in her, she needed excitement and admiration. It was possible Alvin had swept her off her feet, made love to her and promised her a life of romance and excitement if she fled with him.

'I think Romey knows this,' she thought, 'but it makes no difference to me, I still hate her and she must go.'

'As soon as you are strong enough, you must find somewhere to live,' she said, turning away. 'You cannot remain here; you had better return to Spain.'

When she got no answer she glanced at the silent figure in the bed and saw the sudden pinched look and nervous, restless hands.

'I—I *cannot* go to Spain! I haven't any money . . . and I am going to have Alvin': child!'

CHAPTER
TWELVE

'When is the child expected?' Romey asked.

'Some time in February,' Lalia told him.

They were walking in the neglected walled garden where gnarled apple trees and unpruned fruit bushes battled against a tide of weeds. The rose-red bricks of the old walls where cherry and apricot trees had broken from their moorings gave a warmth to the scene and Lalia had chosen the garden in which to tell Romey of Rosa's confession.

'She has told me the truth at last,' she said, gathering up her skirts to avoid a sprawling bramble. 'She begged Alvin to marry her, but he refused. He accused her of behaving unwisely with one of the planters. Rosa says she was innocent, but . . .'

'Even so, to send her back like an unwanted parcel of goods, a woman pregnant with his child!' Romey's face and voice were grim. 'After all, he persuaded her to leave her husband.'

'Yes, I now believe he did,' Lalia admitted. 'I would not allow it at first, but now I think I must. I think she was deeply in love with him, as deeply as a woman of her nature can be, but I wonder if she would have gone so far as to leave my father if Alvin had not demanded it.'

'They would have had an illicit affair for a time, then it would have blown over. Neither of them has the nature to be faithful for long, and your father would probably never have known.'

They walked in silence for a time. Suddenly Lalia said:

'I find it almost impossible to believe Alvin could behave so ruthlessly.'

Romey, walking beside her, his hands clasped behind his back, raised his head.

'The weak can be ruthless when it suits their plans. Rosa, and Jamaica, have been the ruin of Alvin, they have brought out all that is worst in him. Now the question is . . . what do you intend to do?'

His question surprised her; she had expected him to act upon his own judgment of the situation.

'I hardly know yet. I cannot turn her out, she has nowhere to go and no money. And she is not well; she was ill on the journey and the doctor on the steamer told her she should rest and be properly fed. But I cannot have her in the house.'

He looked at her, his dark eyebrows raised enquiringly: 'Then?'

'I have thought about it,' she said slowly. 'Romey, didn't you tell me the tenants of that little house by the bridge had lately left it? It is small but comfortable and is furnished.'

He nodded without speaking, his eyes intent on her face as she went on. 'She could stay until the child is born. I would see she had a maid and a man servant, and we could pay the food bills.'

'You wish her to live in Beech Cottage then, Lalia? You would do that for her?'

'I think I have to,' she sighed. 'I dislike and distrust her, but she *was* my father's wife and he loved her. She betrayed that trust, but I think—I truly feel—he would not wish me to refuse her help now.' She stood still, her face raised to his. 'I obey *his* wish, not mine, I fear. As you said, I am cruel.'

He caught her shoulders, pulling her closer, a curious expression on his face and a glow in his eyes that made her catch her breath.

There's a whole world of romance and history waiting for you...

Take Four Masquerade novels with no risk and no commitment. Discover a world long vanished—a world of chivalry and intrigue, powerful desires and exotic locations, a past that is somehow more real, more gripping, more memorable. Behind the dry, dusty curtain of history are real people, soldiers and statesmen, princesses and serving girls, managing to find true love amid the turmoil that was the Old World all those years ago.

By taking out a subscription to our special Reader Service you can receive four brand new Historical Romances every two months, delivered to your door, postage and packing free. But there's no commitment to buy more books than you want—you can cancel your subscription at any time.

We pride ourselves on our friendly, caring service to readers. You can speak to our editor Nancy Baker with any queries you may have, simply by phoning her on 01-684 2141.

Send the coupon for your Four Free Historical Romances—they are yours to keep, whatever you decide.

The Masquerade Reader Service, P.O. Box 236, Croydon, Surrey CR9 3RU

'So cruel that you would house and feed and care for the woman who nearly wrecked your life! You are indeed a heartless, inhumane creature and I . . . I love you for it!' He released her abruptly. 'I shall see about Beech Cottage at once. Send servants down to clean it, and I'll tell the gardener to see to wood for fires. Has Rosa any luggage?'

'Only a small valise. I shall supply her with what she needs. And I shall ask the doctor to call.'

'She can have the use of the dogcart sometimes so she can take the air, I'll tell Simpson to send it with one of the grooms.'

As they walked back, Romey said: 'I'm going to write to Alvin. I don't expect to get an answer; he's cut all ties with this country and his family. Did he know about the child?'

'Yes, and pretended it was not his.'

He shot her a glance. 'Do you think it is?'

'How can I know?' She drew her shawl closer about her, shivering a little. 'I will have to write to Mrs Prior.'

'You will do no good there either,' he told her, smiling grimly, 'her feelings for Rosa out-match yours.'

They walked back to the house in silence and Lalia sat down to write to Mrs Prior with the conviction that Romey was right and she would get no help from that quarter.

Rosa was delighted with the plans made for her. She became animated and demanded to see the cottage and was full of how she meant to live there.

'Of course I shall need a carriage, or at least a pony-trap,' she said airily. 'The cottage is so isolated. And *one* servant is barely sufficient.'

'You will be taken out for a drive when you wish,' Lalia said, repressing her irritation, 'and you must manage with one servant, Sarah is a good cook and used to housework;

and the man servant will do the heavy work and look after the fires and so on.'

'Well, *I* must not do any work in my condition. Your doctor says I should take some exercise every day, but I do not agree.'

Mrs Prior did not answer Lalia's letter and it was obvious she meant to have nothing to do with Rosa or Alvin's child.

Rosa was installed in Beech Cottage with Sarah and appeared satisfied with arrangements. But she protested angrily at the small allowance she was to receive.

'You have plenty of money, Lalia, and it is money that should be mine!' Her eyes narrowed as she glanced at Lalia sitting beside her in the bright little sitting-room of her new home. 'You cannot have loved Alvin much since you married so soon after. Romey was lucky to find a wealthy woman so easily.'

Lalia rose abruptly. 'Your accounts for food and necessities will be paid regularly, Sarah will give them to me. There is no need for you to spend much money. Goodbye, Rosa. You would be wise to take the doctor's advice and not lie about all day.'

On Romey's advice, Rosa was told she must call herself Mrs Darrencourt. It was possible the local families had not known of the scandal, but it was best to tell people that Rosa was a relation who had returned from abroad to have her child. The servants Lalia had brought from Yorkshire would hold their tongues, she knew.

Mrs Overton and Violet called and Lalia greeted them warmly. They asked for news of Mrs Brookford and she was able to give a good account of her progress and the hope that she would be returning soon. Violet wanted to hear of the exhibitions and fashions of London, and when she and Lalia were alone she remarked that her sister Fanny was being very silly about the new curate and

er mother was considering sending her to an aunt in
Brighton.

Good food and rest had made Rosa bloom and as her
spirits lifted she became restless and inclined to complain
she saw no one and had no social life. Lalia was firm, and
told her she must accept her situation and make the best of
it. She did not remind Rosa what that situation might have
been had she and Romey not allowed her to live in the
cottage, because Rosa saw no reason why someone
should not look after her and showed little gratitude for
what had been done for her. She asked for the dogcart
often as she loved to go driving in the country.

Christmas came and with it, Mrs Brookford, Mrs Grant
and Minnie. The London treatment had been very
successful and Lalia rejoiced in her mother-in-law's
renewed health and freedom from pain. The situation
with Rosa had been explained by letter, and although Mrs
Brookford had no wish to meet the woman whose
conduct she condemned, she agreed that it had been
impossible to turn her out at such a time.

'As long as she does not cause you any more trouble,
dear Lalia,' she said. 'Alvin was very wrong to turn her
away. But she had brought much of her suffering on
herself. Once the child is born I think you must send her
back to Spain, since Mrs Prior will not help.'

'Yes, she certainly cannot stay here for ever.'

Malcolm Overton had been away when Lalia returned
to Dorset. Now he had returned and she met him when
she and Romey dined at Stonewell Court. She was
wearing her purple gown and her mother's amethyst
necklet and earrings and Minnie had arranged her fair
curls high on her head with a few curls falling at the back.
She smiled at Malcolm as she asked him how he had
enjoyed his visit to Italy.

As they talked, she was amused and a little intrigued to
find his manner more mature and his self-possession

increased. He had acquired a touch of sophistication and was more reserved than she remembered him. Suspecting the cause, she probed with what she considered discreetly veiled curiosity and was somewhat put out when he looked at her squarely and said, 'Oh yes, I fell in love when I was in Italy, that is what you wish to know, isn't it Mrs Brookford?'

'Certainly not,' she said hastily, aware of her colour rising. 'I should not dream of asking . . . or wishing to know . . .' she looked up and caught the laughter in his eyes and cried: 'Oh, you wretched creature! You are laughing at me! For punishment you shall tell me who she was and how badly your heart is damaged.'

'Certainly—since it is hardly damaged at all,' he vowed, and told her of the pretty Italian widow whose experience in the art of love was greater, Lalia guessed, than his.

On the drive back Romey remarked: 'Young Malcolm has lost his milk-teeth, Italy has developed him, it would appear. He's improved.'

'He has become an attractive young man,' Lalia agreed.

'And has got over his calf love for you, I see,' Romey's voice held amusement. 'I deplore his taste, but must admit I feel easier now that he won't try to kidnap you.'

Lalia smiled in the darkness. Something in Malcolm's eyes and manner made her suspect that his calf love might have been replaced by a more manly and deeper feeling. She told herself she liked Malcolm and it would do no harm, and perhaps be an antidote to the widow, if he were to fall in love—very slightly, of course—with her.

December blew itself out in a series of wintry gales and sleet dashing against the windows of Hildon Manor, and all work on the outside had to be halted. Inside, walls were papered, panelling repaired, ceilings painted and kitchen flagstones made even. Mrs Grant complained of the workmen getting in her way, but admitted the result was worth all the trouble. She had made no comment when Lalia had told her of Rosa and her condition except to say: 'I'll not say a word, nor will James.'

Rosa, resenting her cumbersome figure and restricted activities, was becoming peevish and Lalia visited her less often. She was physically well, but her shallow nature found no way in which to occupy itself and she complained at her hard luck in not being able to ride or drive the dogcart.

'I am perfectly sure the doctor is wrong and I *could* drive the cart,' she told Lalia who had called one morning when the winds had dropped and the skies were clear for the first time in a week. 'I am used to driving, Alvin kept a smart little outfit in Jamaica and I always drove it.'

'You must certainly do no such thing now.'

'Silverstone estate was very pleasant, you know,' Rosa remarked, lying back against her cushions. 'We had a lot of servants. They were impertinent sometimes and we weren't allowed to whip them. I think it a great pity the slaves were freed, it has only spoilt them. They left the plantations and had nowhere to go and many went to live in the hills and became quite wild and troublesome. Some time ago there was a horrid attack on an estate and the planter was murdered.' She shifted her heavy body restlessly. 'Our house was pretty, it had a wide verandah all around and louvre-windows and a fine carved stairway. But there was little society and Alvin would not let me entertain. Sir John Peter Grant gave parties at Government House, but I was never invited.'

There had been no answer from Alvin. Romey's friend who was in the sugar-importing business mentioned in a letter that Alvin Prior had been ill with a low fever and was taking time to recover.

'If he is still drinking, it won't help him,' was Romey's only comment.

Because of the weather, nothing could be done to the workers' cottages, but Lalia had sent a midwife to see to the ailing infant and had supplied food and clothes to the household. Romey had increased his men's wages, which did not make him popular with his neighbours, something that did not worry him in the slightest. Mrs Brookford, Lalia and Mrs Grant sewed garments for the children and many a bowl of soup and packet of sugar and tea found its way into the poorer families' kitchens.

One morning Lalia decided to drive to the village and sent for the dogcart, only to be told Mrs Darrencourt had asked for it.

'Then I will take the landau,' she told Simpson. She saw the man hesitate and added: 'Is anything wrong, Simpson?'

He looked down at the cap in his hands. 'Well, in a manner o' speaking, it is, Ma'am. Seems as if the lady has took a notion she'm like to drive the trap and young Jock zays he's a testy time wi' her to stop her taking up the reins.'

'She mustn't drive, Simpson,' Lalia exclaimed in alarm, 'tell Jock he must never let her!'

'Aye, 'tis what I tell he, but he'm young and frighted to offend the lady.'

'Then you must send one of the older men who will be firm with Mrs Darrencourt, and I will speak to her myself.'

''Twill be best . . .' A sudden sound made them both look up as a horse ridden recklessly charged up to where they stood on the steps of the house. A boy hurled himself off, his face white and his voice shaking as he gasped out, 'She'm took the cart! She axed me to get her another cushion and when I comes back she'm gone a-racing down the road, whipping poor Jenny unmerciful! She took the corner crooky-crazy an' a wheel cotched in a fence pole an' . . . an' she were thrown out when cart tippled over!'

'Oh, dear God!' Lalia's face blanched. 'Is she much hurt? Did you leave her there? Someone must go at once—'

'Happened Doctor Green were a-coming down road and we takes her back to the house.' Jock paused to get his breath. 'Sarah and him be minding her now.'

'Where is your master? He must be told!' She turned to Simpson. 'Bring the carriage at once while I fetch Mrs Grant.'

As she ran into the hall, Romey came from the morning-room. Quickly she told him what had happened and let him take charge with a thankful heart. Mrs Grant soon gathered what she needed and they drove rapidly down the avenue and along to the cottage that stood above the bridge.

Doctor Green met them at the door. 'She has had a bad fall, Mrs Brookford. What in heaven's name made her do a mad thing like that?'

'She wanted to drive herself . . . I warned her not to, I forbade it. How is she, Doctor?'

'It was lucky I was on my way to visit her and we got her into bed in time.'

'In time for what?' Romey asked sharply.

'In time for her child, a girl, to be born,' Doctor Green said.

'The child is born? Lalia felt Romey's arm go around her as she swayed. 'And she? Is she . . . Will she be all right?'

The doctor's eyes went from her to Romey and he said gently. 'I am distressed to tell you, no.'

'You mean . . .'

He bowed his head. 'I am afraid Mrs Darrencourt will not last the night.'

CHAPTER
THIRTEEN

THE end came just as the night lifted its veil in the east, allowing the first rosy blush to warm the sky.

Lalia, sitting white-faced and tense at the bedside, saw the great dark eyes open suddenly and fix upon her. Rosa's blanched lips moved and Lalia bent forward to catch the whispered words that came on a faint breath from the dying woman.

'I . . . am sorry . . . about your father . . .' the breath rattled ominously in her throat. 'Alvin . . .' she murmured, and was still.

Mrs Grant's arms lifted Lalia from her chair. 'Come away, Miss Lalia dear, the poor creature's gone, God rest her soul.'

Romey was waiting outside. He came forward, glanced at the housekeeper, and slid his arm around Lalia, supporting her as she burst into a storm of weeping.

'I—I did not like her! I hated her once. But that this should happen to her! Poor Rosa, she was so alive, and now . . .'

'Come home, my dear, you can do no more here.' He picked her up and carried her to the carriage. He did not speak on the journey back, but the comfort of his arm around her gave her the strength she needed and slowly her tears stopped and she leaned wearily on his shoulder as she whispered, 'What made her do such a thing? She knew she was getting near her time. I should have suspected something, Romey; she said more than once that she wanted to drive the dogcart.'

'No one could guess she would do such a wild thing. I think she was a woman fated to destroy herself. You did all you could for her, Lalia, and that was much.'

A bright fire blazed in the morning-room and she sank gratefully into the chair Romey pulled forward. He brought a chair for himself and after giving an order to James, sat beside her, chafing her cold hands.

James entered softly with a tray. 'The brandy, sir, and I thought Madam might like a biscuit.'

'Thank you, James.' She tried to smile, seeing the distress in his face.

He cleared his throat. 'We are all much shocked at the tragedy, Madam. I would like to offer our sympathy. Is there anything else, sir? Minnie has prepared Madam's bed should she wish to rest.'

'Thank you, James, that will be all.'

Slowly the state of shock wore off and Lalia was able to think more clearly. Rosa's mother must be notified, if it was possible. Suddenly she sat up with a gasp.

'The baby! I had forgotten about her! Romey, what are we going to do? She may die!'

'I think not. The doctor said she is strong despite her premature arrival, and he will take her to a farmer's wife who has just lost her own baby and is willing to be a wet-nurse. He and Mrs Grant have made the arrangement and the baby is with the woman now.'

'Oh, thank God for that! But she must be christened and the birth registered . . . They will ask for details of the father and . . . What must we do, Romey?'

'The truth will have to come out,' he said, his hands tightening on hers, 'it cannot hurt her now.'

'But the child? Mrs Prior will have nothing to do with her, and Rosa's mother, too, may refuse to take her. And Alvin will do nothing.'

'You must write to Rosa's mother, Mrs Carew, and tell

her everything. The lawyer will have her address. It is for her to decide.'

Mrs Brookford came and took Lalia upstairs and persuaded her to rest, and her loving sympathy and gentleness warmed Lalia's chilled heart.

'Dear Mother Edith, you are a very great comfort to me,' she said.

'I am glad, my dear. You have so often comforted and cared for me. Now you must rest and try to sleep a little.'

The weeks that followed were a strain for Lalia. The shock of Rosa's death and anxiety for the baby brought her a depression of spirit she tried to overcome, but without success. Romey was with her often and one morning, some days after the funeral, she remarked,

'You are at home much more now, but I know you have work to do and you must not stay here because of me, you know.'

He was standing by the window and turned at her words to smile at her.

'And if I wish to stay at home with you, would it be so strange? You are sad and your spirits are low. When I see you smiling and colour in your cheeks—and when you begin to argue with me and defy me—well, then I shall no doubt be driven out of the house.'

She laughed for the first time in days. 'You make me sound a shrew!'

'And you make me out a bully,' he teased her. 'We are a fine couple.' He glanced out of the window. 'Ah, the post has come. I wonder . . .' He strode from the room and returned a moment later with a letter which he gave to Lalia saying, 'It comes from Spain.'

Mrs Carew's English was poor and her letter somewhat smudged. She could hardly believe, she wrote, that her darling Rosa could have behaved in such a manner! If it was true, her daughter had indeed disgraced her husband's and her own family's name, but the tragedy of her death was hard to bear, her eldest and most beautiful daughter . . . such a loss would sadden her heart for ever. There were many such protestations of anguish from which emerged one fact: Mrs Carew, struggling to provide for herself and her daughters on a pittance, was in no position to take Rosa's baby. The father must provide, or his family.

Lalia gave the letter to Romey and watched him read it. When he had finished it, he looked at her with his dark brows lifted in enquiry.

'We will get no help there. What do you plan to do now?'

Lalia rose, her lassitude falling away now she knew she had come to a time of decision.

'I shall take the child, if you agree. There is no one else; she is unwanted, poor little creature. I never wished to see Rosa again, or have any involvement with the past, but I cannot let her child be thrust into an orphanage or . . . Romey,' she went to him swiftly, 'will you agree? I cannot do this without your permission.'

He did not speak for some minutes, but stood looking at her with a curious expression on his strong, dark face. At last he said, 'How you have changed, Lalia. Once, you would have thrown Rosa out and cared very little what became of her child.'

She winced. 'I am glad if I have indeed changed. I think you married a rather selfish, vain and unkind woman.'

'And now find myself with a wife with a loving heart. But I wish—' he stopped quickly and turned away.

'What do you wish?'

He made an abrupt gesture. 'Never mind, perhaps I'll tell you one day. I'll see Doctor Green and make arrangements about the baby. It must be christened; have you thought of a name?'

'Rosa?'

He shook his head. 'Did she have another name?'

Lalia wrinkled her brow in thought. 'I think she did. Yes, she once told me her father wanted her to have an English name and insisted on Elizabeth.'

'That will do. Call upon the Vicar and arrange for the christening in a few weeks' time. Doctor Green tells me the baby is getting on well.'

The neighbours were discreet in their expression of sympathy. Only to Violet Overton did Lalia reveal the whole story.

'We knew something of it,' Violet confessed. 'Some friends in Yorkshire told my mother about your father's unfortunate marriage and the disaster that followed. And *your* unhappiness, dear Lalia. But let us talk of happier things. Will you ride with me again? The weather has improved, but it may not be for long and we should take advantage of the dry spell while it lasts.'

Lalia agreed gladly. She was feeling the need for exercise and of getting out of the house. Recent rain and high winds had kept her indoors and she chafed at her inactivity. She sent a message to Simpson to bring her mare out next morning.

She was not totally surprised to see Malcolm riding with his sister to meet her. He greeted her with a smile and suggested they rode over to Stonewell Court after they had had a gallop.

The ride across fields still sodden with rain brought a becoming flush to Lalia's cheeks and a glow to her eyes and she felt the blood course through her in a feeling of well-being she had missed since Rosa's death. Slightly to her surprise, Malcolm did not try to stay close to her as he had formerly done. His calf-love had certainly evaporated, she thought with a touch of pique, and perhaps she had been mistaken in imagining it had been replaced by something more mature. He certainly did not seem particularly aware of her this morning.

Mrs Overton made her welcome and refreshments were sent for while they chatted.

'Will you ride with us tomorrow morning, Mrs Brookford?' Malcolm asked. 'Violet has missed her morning gallops over the hills.'

'And have *you* missed them?' The moment she had spoken, she regretted her words. They sounded cheaply flirtatious and she felt herself grow hot, knowing the change in his behaviour had slightly piqued her.

'Of course I have,' he said coolly. 'Our gallops were good sport and I trust we may have more of them.'

That night, when Lalia was sitting with her mother-in-law and Romey in the parlour, she looked up from her needlework to remark, 'I noticed someone has taken Belmont, that charming house about a mile outside the village. There are curtains up and furniture was being taken in. Do you know who comes there, Romey?'

He looked up from his book. 'A Lady Grenfell from Kent, a widow.'

His mother sat up abruptly. 'Surely that cannot be Edwina Grenfell? I think I heard her husband had died last year—but no doubt I am wrong and it is not she.'

Romey shut his book and rose, stretching himself before the fire.

'Yes, it is Edwina. I had a note from her a few days ago telling me she had rented the house for a year. Excuse my leaving you, I have some letters to write.' He went out of the room.

His mother's eyes followed him and Lalia, who was watching her curiously, asked, 'Do you know this Lady Grenfell?'

Mrs Brookford did not answer at once; when she did, she kept her eyes on the sewing in her lap.

'Yes, she and her family were near us when we lived in Kent, before my husband inherited Hildon Manor.

Edwina was an extremely beautiful girl, but a little wild, I used to think.'

'I suppose Romey knew her well also,' Lalia remarked and was surprised to see a faint colour rise in her mother-in-law's cheeks.

'Yes, he did. I think you had better know that she and Romey were engaged to marry, but she threw him over for an older, very wealthy man. It is curious she should have decided to come to Dorset. I wish she had not.'

'Oh, I expect it was just chance,' Lalia said lightly. 'It will be pleasant for her to know someone here.'

Mrs Brookford shook her head slowly. 'I wish she had not come.'

CHAPTER
FOURTEEN

LALIA had written to Mrs Prior to tell her of Rosa's death and the birth of Alvin's daughter, but, as she had expected, she got no answer. Little Elizabeth was going on well, but the wet-nurse's milk was beginning to fail and Doctor Green decided the baby should be weaned by the end of March. Minnie had a sister Kate, who had been with a London family as under-nurse but who had disliked living in a city and had returned to Dorset. Lalia sent for Kate and finding her a healthy, well-mannered girl, engaged her to look after Elizabeth.

A room had been prepared as a nursery. Sometimes Lalia wondered if she had been wise to take Rosa's daughter. Neither she nor Romey wished to adopt her, but they would have to look after Elizabeth for as long as she was with them, and as she grew up this might bring problems.

Lalia, kept busy with preparations for taking little Elizabeth, did not have time to find out more about the new tenant of Belmont. Mrs Brookford had not mentioned Lady Grenfell again and Lalia did not like to ask for more information. But she spoke of their new neighbour to Romey, asking when she was to arrive and when it would be proper for her to call.

'Your mother tells me you knew Lady Grenfell's family in Kent,' she remarked, and wondered if he would mention the engagement.

He nodded. 'Yes, the families saw a lot of each other at that time. It is not necessary for you to call since you are in mourning.'

'Oh, I think it would look strange if I did not,' she glanced at him as he stood in the doorway, waiting to ride off on Blackie who was tossing his bridle peevishly, 'since you once knew her so well. Perhaps your mother will come with me.'

He tapped his riding boot lightly with his crop, as if impatient to be away.

'You will find Mother is not over-fond of Edwina, I'm afraid. I shan't tell you why because you know perfectly well, I can see it in the amazingly innocent expression you are wearing.' He grinned mockingly. 'You cannot take me in, Lalia, I know you too well.'

'That is a dangerous thing to say,' she retorted, 'it might incite me to see if I *can* deceive you!'

'Try—it will be an interesting experiment.' He raised his crop in salute and ran down the steps.

She watched him go, her eyes thoughtful. If Edwina had broken his heart it would appear to have mended successfully. There was a curious parallel in her and Romey's experiences, he, too, had known disloyalty and rejection and had no faith in, or need of, love. A marriage based on friendship, respect and affection was what she and Romey wanted, probably for the same reason.

'I certainly have done with love,' she thought as she went into the house. 'My father's love for Rosa proved fatal, Alvin's love for Rosa ended in cruel desertion, and Rosa's love for him . . .' she heard again the last faint whisper, 'Alvin . . .' and knew Rosa had truly loved the man who had persuaded her to abandon home and husband and then deserted her. Love was a trap and the risks of disloyalty, treachery and heartbreak were too great.

'What Romey and I have is much the safest, most comfortable and satisfying attachment,' she told herself, 'and I want no other.'

March winds blustered their way across the countryside, raging through the plantations of firs and tossing the bare branches of beech and oak. Winter was fighting a bitter battle before retreating under the onslaught of spring and the country suffered uprooted trees, broken branches and rivers overspilling their banks.

The work inside Hildon Manor was done and Lalia walked through the newly-decorated rooms with a joyful feeling that spring had come to the house, even if it was late in renewing the countryside.

Neighbourhood news percolated through visitors: the Overtons had gone to London for two weeks; two families in the neighbourhood were suffering from the influenza; the new tenant of Belmont was not to arrive until the end of March and was reputed to be bringing her London staff with her.

Baby Elizabeth came to Hildon Manor on a day when a thin sun was piercing the clouds and Lalia felt it was a good omen. Kate was installed in the rooms upstairs allotted to a nursery suite and when Lalia watched her settle the baby in her cot before preparing her bottle, she knew that she had chosen a girl she could rely on to care for Rosa's daughter.

'She is a pretty baby,' she told Romey that evening, 'you must see her.'

He shrugged as he poured himself out a whisky and soda. 'I'm not a judge of babies. Are you happy to have her here?' His gaze was direct and searching. 'You have taken on a great responsibility.'

'Yes, but I am prepared to take it. And you know, it *is* possible that Alvin may have a change of heart. He *must* feel guilty about Rosa and the baby; he will acknowledge her one day, I think.'

Romey said nothing for a moment, then, taking his drink over to the fire, he stood with his foot on the fender staring down into the leaping flames.

'You take a more charitable view than I. I very much

doubt if he can feel anything—guilt, remorse or a desire to acknowledge responsibility, now.'

'Have you heard something, then?' she asked quickly.

'I am told he is a sick man.'

Lalia was surprised at the pleasure she found in watching Elizabeth's progress. Kate reported her weaning as being quite exceptionally successful.

'She's a dear little thing, Ma'am, and as good as gold. A sweet nature and doing well despite being so early-born.'

The morning visits to the nursery began to have a charm for Lalia, and Mrs Brookford, too, often found her way up to the nursery.

'I see a likeness to Alvin, I think,' she told Lalia, 'he was a lovely baby.' She sighed. 'But I hope she does not inherit his nature.'

The Overtons returned and Mrs Overton called at Belmont and reported on her visit when she came to Hildon Manor. Malcolm accompanied her and was carried off by Romey to see the new pony-landau he had bought, leaving the ladies to sit before the tea table and gossip comfortably.

Lalia was wearing a grey velvet dress trimmed with mauve braid and with a cream silk inset at the neck. The skirt was caught back to show the pretty lines of her body and Mrs Overton remarked on her charming appearance.

'You choose such pretty, feminine clothes, my dear,' she said. 'I cannot say I care for this new idea of tailored costumes; we saw some in London and they have a hard, masculine look when worn with a shirt blouse and tie and, sometimes, a waistcoat. But I am afraid Fanny was quite taken with them.'

Lalia laughed as she refilled her guest's cup. 'We may hate the fashion, but I expect we shall all adopt it and declare it delightful! Now pray tell me about your call at Belmont and how you found Lady Grenfell.'

'She is quite charming; graceful, easy manners with a

lively and intelligent mind,' Mrs Overton said enthusiastically, 'and she is really beautiful! A skin like a young girl, and such huge, soft grey eyes—sometimes they appear quite green. It is sad to see so young and lovely a woman widowed.'

'Do you know anything of her late husband?'

'Very little. My husband says he was very much older than she, and of course he was very wealthy. Her house is beautifully furnished and she has filled the stables and has a landau and a fine carriage and a large staff of servants.'

'My husband knew her and her family some years ago,' Lalia said. 'I look forward to meeting her.'

'Oh, you certainly must call. As a matter of fact, she asked about you. It appears she did not know Mr Brookford had married as she and her husband had been living abroad.'

That evening Lalia told Romey she intended to call on Lady Grenfell.

'I feel it is only right, as she is a neighbour. Mrs Overton says she is very beautiful.'

'Yes, she was always beautiful.' Was there a faint change in his voice, Lalia wondered, or had she imagined it? 'I don't think you will have much in common. She is much in society; this is her latest whim, to become a countrywoman, and I don't expect it to last.'

'I suppose she has enough money to indulge her whims,' Lalia said.

'Sir Conrad was a wealthy man, he was wise enough to invest in railways. How is Elizabeth getting on?'

Lalia jumped up. 'Come and see her. She is sweet, and so good-natured. Kate quite loves her.'

Elizabeth had just finished her supper and smiled charmingly at them before falling asleep. Romey grinned at her as she lay in the lace-trimmed cot.

'What a comic little scrap of humanity.'

'I wish Rosa could have seen her,' Lalia said impulsively.

He nodded without speaking and, taking her arm, led her from the room.

'You are enjoying having her here, Lalia?'

'Yes, I am,' she replied. 'It is rewarding to see her grow and develop. Of course, I suppose it is not like having a child of one's own . . .' She broke off abruptly. She and Romey would never have a child.

'I do not want one,' she thought, feeling her nerves tense, 'and neither does Romey.' She looked at him as he walked beside her, wondering what lay behind his reserved expression. She thought she knew him, but did she? A sudden expression crossing his face, a look in his eyes, an unexpected remark, sometimes startled her, reminding her uncomfortably how little she really knew of him. Once again she found herself speculating on his former love for Edwina Grenfell. He spoke of her casually, almost indifferently, but Romey did not give his feelings away.

'What deep thoughts are making you frown?' his voice made her start.

'I was thinking how little I really knew you.'

To her surprise she saw his mouth tighten for a moment.

'You knew enough of me to marry me.'

'Oh, of course I *do* know you, only sometimes . . .' she shrugged. 'After all, we have not been married for so very long.'

'Are you regretting our marriage?' She was dismayed at the harshness in his voice. They had reached the hall and he stood facing her, his eyes suddenly cold and bleak. 'I am aware it was a poor bargain for you: your fortune for the doubtful honour of bearing my name.'

'Oh Romey, don't be so—so unreasonable,' she burst out, speaking quickly to hide a stab of uneasiness. 'You know I am content. I am happy here, your mother is kind, and now I have Elizabeth to give me an added interest.'

'I wonder if you will grow to love her?' For a second she seemed to feel his eyes burning hers. 'But perhaps you do not love easily, or ever! Yours is an enviable state, Lalia!' He swung around and she did not see him again that evening.

During his mother's visit, Malcolm had asked Lalia if a ride to the coast with him and his sister would interest her and she had agreed she would enjoy it, and it had been arranged they meet on the coast road at ten o'clock on Friday. She forgot about it until Friday morning when she had to change her morning gown hastily for her riding habit and give orders for her mare to be brought around.

It was a bright day with a clear sky and a softness in the air that raised her heart as she rode down the avenue. Romey was away on business in Yeovil and was to stay the night there.

When she came to the turning to the Overton estate she was surprised to see Malcolm waiting alone.

'I regret to tell you Violet has a bad sore throat and Mama will not allow her out,' he said cheerfully as Lalia rode up. 'She is greatly disappointed and hopes you will not allow it to spoil our ride to the sea. It is a beautiful day and much too good to waste indoors.'

Lalia hesitated. Strictly, it was not quite proper for young Mrs Brookford to spend the morning riding with an attractive young bachelor. But it *was* a lovely day and something in the sunlight and clear air was making her reckless. Her mare was mettlesome and eager for a gallop, and the last weeks had proved so windy and wet that it had not been possible to ride much. It was unlikely anyone would see them, and if they did . . .

'Who cares what people think?' Malcolm said softly and smiled at her startled expression. 'Oh, I know what makes you hesitate, but such thoughts are out of place on a day like this. Come, let us be going or our horses will take us willy-nilly.'

The swift movement, the feel of the horse's muscles beneath her, the rush of sea-wind in her face made Lalia cast all cares away as they rode. After all, she was a married woman and Malcolm was a mere boy . . . Then she remembered the mere boy was four years older than she. What matter? To go riding with a friend was quite unexceptional and she was being ridiculous even to question the propriety of such an action.

When they came to the cliffs, Malcolm found a narrow track down to the beach which was strewn with debris flung up by a recent storm. Lalia's lips parted to breathe in the delicious salt air, her eyes alight as she followed Malcolm in a canter along the sand. As she came up to him he said, looking at her flushed and radiant in her dark-blue riding habit and cream stock and veil-trimmed hat. 'How lovely you are, more lovely than I remember . . . and I thought you the most beautiful woman I'd seen then.'

'Thank you, Mr Overton.' Her words were formal, but her eyes had a mischievous light. 'It is only the well-known benefit of sea air upon the female complexion.'

'You like to tease me. Do you think to put me off paying you compliments? Every beautiful woman is entitled to compliments.'

'Of course,' she said carelessly, 'they are lightly given and soon forgotten.'

'Mine are not lightly given.' At his words she turned her head to look at him and something in his eyes made her pull on her reins and say as casually as she could, 'I think it is time we returned, it is near noon.'

'Why will you not let me tell you how lovely I think you are?' He persisted, putting out his hand to hold her reins. 'Are you afraid I might tell you—'

'I am afraid you might be silly enough to tell me

something we both might regret,' she said coolly, although her heart was beating faster than normal. 'Come, I wish to return. I have to go out visiting this afternoon.'

She turned her mare and set off along the beach. As they drew near the path up to the cliff she saw an old, black-shawled woman poking through the wrack left by the high tides. The woman straightened up as she heard their approach and pushed back strands of dark hair from a wrinkled face that might have been carved from mahogany. Dark eyes glittered as she stepped forward, holding up a clawlike hand and making the mare shy nervously.

'Stay my beauty, let old Nan tell your fortune! Gi' me silver on my hand and I'll tell 'ee secrets of the future, aye and of the past. I've a girt power in me, Lady. I've the gift.'

'Be off with you!' Malcolm said angrily, 'you frighten the horses.'

'I'll quiet 'em, sir.' She began to chant a wailing tune in a high, cracked voice and both horses pricked their ears as they stilled their restless movements. The woman laughed.

'I've the gift wi' animals, and wi' the future. Come, lady, let Nan find your fortune in your hand and face.'

'Out of the way—' Malcolm began, but Lalia broke in, saying.

'Let her tell my fortune, I have never had it told before.' She felt in her pocket and found a shilling which she threw to the woman who snatched it and hid it swiftly in the folds of her dirty gown.

'Come, Lady, gi' me your hand.' Lalia winced as she felt the dry claw grasp her bare fingers and she half wished she had not stopped. Malcolm sat, smiling tolerantly, flicking his horse lightly with his whip.

'You'll get a fine lot of nonsense for your money, Mrs Brookford,' he mocked her.

The woman was muttering to herself. Suddenly her words came more clearly and Lalia, at first impatient, found herself listening with unwilling intentness.

'There's been a cruel act . . . ah, your pride's been beaten down, my lady, but not your heart.'

'What do you see of the future,' Lalia asked quickly.

'There's girt trouble for you,' the woman said slowly, raising her head to stare at Lalia. 'You will tell a lie—and regret it wi' pain and tears! I see a hot sun . . .' she was staring past Lalia with a fixed expression in her dark eyes. 'No tree standing . . . and danger!' She seemed to shrink into herself, her head bowed and her face hidden. 'Go your ways, I can tell 'ee no more . . . But be careful of the knife! The great knife . . .'

Lalia whipped up her horse, trying to shake off the curious feeling of panic the woman's words had aroused. Malcolm had been right, she should not have listened to her. She heard Malcolm say as they rode up the track to the cliff,

'You are quite white! Damn that old witch, she's upset you! Would you like to stop and rest?'

'Oh no,' Lalia tried to smile but found her face stiff. 'I am not upset. She was talking a lot of nonsense and of course I don't believe any of it.'

'Of course not, what can an old fool like that know of the future?'

'What can anyone know of their future?' She shivered suddenly and felt his hand upon her arm.

'The future is what we make of it,' he said with quiet intensity. 'We get what we strive for if we strive long enough.' She tried to tear her eyes away from his but failed. The look on his face was that of a man, not a love-sick boy. 'I know what I want most in this world.'

'No—I will not listen to you!' She jerked her arm free and urged the mare on. Once out on the cliffs, she set the pace and did not look at him until she bade him a cool goodbye before riding on to Hildon Manor. It had been a mistake to ride with him; she had not seriously supposed he was attracted to her; she would be more careful in future.

The future . . . what was it the old woman had said about a lie? She tried to remember as she rode up to the house, but all she heard was a hoarse voice muttering: 'Be careful of the knife . . . the great knife!'

CHAPTER
FIFTEEN

To pay a call upon Lady Grenfell would, Lalia decided, help to take her mind off the unpleasant occurrence of the morning. As well as the old woman's disturbing words, there was much in Malcolm's behaviour that made her uneasy. His words and his look had been passionate, as if he had tried to conceal his feelings and failed. It was flattering to her vanity that he should find her beautiful and desirable, but he must not be encouraged. She liked him and it would be sad if she had to dismiss him from her company; she knew she would miss him.

She ordered the landau and after seeing her mother-in-law settled for her rest and a short visit to the nursery, she went to dress for her call upon Lady Grenfell. Minnie brought out a grey wool gown, but a sudden impulse made Lalia say, 'Not the grey, Minnie, I will wear my new dress. The year of my mourning is nearly up and I am weary of grey and lavender.'

'Oh yes, Ma'am, you'll look beautiful in the blue, 'tis the colour of your eyes,' Minnie said enthusiastically as she returned the grey gown to the cupboard and brought out the dress that had been ordered from the London modiste who created Lalia's wardrobe for her. The deep sapphire blue velvet of the bodice was elegantly frogged with navy braid and the darker blue skirt, worn without a bustle as was the newest fashion, had the fullness drawn back lower down with a small train. When she had put on her sealskin jacket and hat, Lalia looked at herself in the glass and wryly recognised the impulse that had caused her to dress in a fashion difficult for Lady Grenfell to excel.

Lady Grenfell was at home and received her guest in a charming room, free from the usual heavy draping of windows and mantelpiece and cumbersome furniture upholstered in dark colours. Sunlight flowed in through the windows and lit the pretty flowered carpet and leaf-green walls and the crystal bowls of daffodils.

As Lalia entered, Lady Grenfell rose from her chair and advanced to meet her, smiling, and Lalia saw that she was indeed a beautiful woman with a slim, elegant figure and soft, husky voice.

'How do you do, Mrs Brookford, it is most kind of you to call.' Her large grey eyes had odd flecks of green in them and were shadowed by long lashes. 'I had hoped to meet you, but I heard you were still in mourning.'

'The period is over,' Lalia said, sinking into the chair she was offered. 'I wanted to welcome you to Dorset, especially since I believe you already know my husband and his family.'

'Oh yes, our families saw much of each other when I lived in Kent,' Lady Grenfell said, 'but I have seen and heard nothing of them since my marriage; my husband and I lived much in Italy and France. I had hoped to meet your mother-in-law again, but I am told she is delicate.'

Lalia hastened to give a somewhat exaggerated account of Mrs Brookford's delicate constitution and was relieved to be able to drop the subject when a footman and maid brought in the tea.

She was aware she was being closely inspected; the beautiful grey-green eyes were taking in her looks and her clothes and she was glad she had put on the new dress and her best bronze kid boots with the frivolous high heels.

Her hostess was in green checked taffeta, the plain bodice showing off her figure admirably. Emeralds gleamed in her ears and on her fingers and her bronze hair, arranged high on her head, glowed as the sun caught it.

They spoke of neighbours. Mrs Overton, Lady Grenfell remarked lightly, was quite charming.

'A true countrywoman, occupied with household and family affairs. Her son is good-looking, isn't he? And the elder daughter is quite pretty, I met her with her mother this morning in the village.'

'You met Violet?' Lalia asked, surprised. 'I was told . . . I understood she was kept in the house because of a sore throat.'

Lady Grenfell laughed. 'There was no sign of it when I met her. She remarked on the pleasant weather and said she had been disappointed in a plan to ride that morning.'

Lalia drank her tea thoughtfully. So Malcolm had engineered their being alone on the ride to the sea. It was very wrong of him and she would certainly tell him so. She looked up to see her hostess's eyes on her.

'I was quite anxious to meet you, Mrs Brookford,' she said, her full red lips curving in a smile. 'I did not know Romey had married. It would have been sad had he not—and I should have felt somewhat guilty, I fear.'

Lalia put down her cup, suddenly alert to the change in Lady Grenfell's expression. The eyes were very green now, and had a mischievous light and Lalia stiffened, her own eyes abruptly cool and wary. Attack was always the best defence and she knew now that Lady Grenfell was no friend.

'You mean your engagement to Romey long ago?' she asked, and saw the flash of irritation in the green eyes. 'One often mistakes one's emotions when young.'

'There was no mistake in Romey's attachment to me,' Lady Grenfell said sharply.

'Which you could not return, unfortunately,' Lalia's voice and expression were deceptively tranquil, but inwardly she felt a stir of anger, 'since you broke off the engagement to marry Sir Conrad Grenfell.'

'I had a girlish infatuation for Romey which I mistook for the grand passion. His ardour quite swept me off my feet for a time, before I realised my mistake.'

'And realised your passion for Sir Conrad,' Lalia said, smiling guilelessly. 'I hope your marriage was happy.'

'Divinely so.' Lady Grenfell spoke shortly, a faint frown creasing her smooth forehead. 'He was excessively devoted to me, and I was perfectly prostrated at his unexpected death.' She raised a scrap of lace-trimmed linen to her eyes for a moment.

'Oh, naturally,' Lalia agreed smoothly. 'Let us speak of happier things. Do you intend to remain long in Dorset?'

'It will depend on how much my life here amuses me,' she said carelessly. 'I have not lived much in the country. I was told Dorset is healthy and the scenery pretty. I expect I shall entertain some of my friends from time to time, and of course my neighbours too. You must dine with me soon, Mrs Brookford, Romey and I will have *so* many things to talk of and so many memories to revive.'

'And I shall be delighted to listen to the revival,' Lalia assured her as she pulled her fur jacket about her shoulders. 'I really must be going as Romey is away tonight and I do not wish to leave Mrs Brookford alone for too long.'

Lady Grenfell's slender brows rose. 'So he is not at home today?' She laughed softly and Lalia instinctively braced herself, warned by a sixth sense. 'Ah, so that is why Mr Malcolm Overton does not wish his sister to ride with him this morning! Oh, but do not heed my naughty gossip! Although I could not help thinking it a little strange to see you and the attractive Malcolm Overton ride past when I was in my garden. Romey is devoted to riding, he and I used to ride every day in Kent. But of course, if he was away, he could not accompany you.'

'Yes, he is away,' Lalia's eyes were cold as ice, 'and I

went riding with Malcolm Overton and his sister did not come with us. How fortunate you should be in your garden this morning, since you like gossip, Lady Grenfell. But it *could* be a dangerous and unpopular amusement, you know.'

Lady Grenfell smiled sweetly as the footman appeared at the door.

'But I live for amusement, dear Mrs Brookford. I am a complete hedonist, I'm afraid. You must forgive me.'

Lalia bowed and murmured her thanks and farewell and went out attended by the footman and was driven home in a state of suppressed anger and disgust. So Lady Grenfell was a mischief-maker, as well as a gossip. It was all too obvious she intended to stress her part in Romey's past, either from idle amusement or some less admirable motive.

'I believe she resents Romey having married,' she thought. 'She would have liked to think of him dying for love of her. She is the type of spoilt beauty who cannot imagine any man forgetting her.' But it would be as well to tell Romey at once about her ride to the sea; if he heard it from another quarter he might think she had tried to hide it. *Had* she intended to hide it? She wondered a little uneasily if she would have said anything had not Lady Grenfell been strolling so inopportunely in her garden that morning.

Romey came back early next morning and joined Lalia at breakfast.

'Work can begin on the cottages any time now,' he remarked. 'They are in a bad way after this rain.'

'I am glad. There are letters for you, Romey, is there anything from Alvin?'

'No, I have had no news of him lately. Is little Elizabeth well?'

She was able to assure him the baby was blooming.

'I called at Belmont yesterday,' she told him.

'And how did you find Edwina?'

'She is a very lovely woman, and her house is charming,' she said carefully, 'but I think she dislikes me.'

He had risen and was about to leave the room, but turned to look at her. 'Why do you say that?'

She hesitated, but only for a moment. It was ridiculous that she could not mention the past to Romey, her husband.

'I think she would like to believe you stayed unwed because you were once engaged to her.'

'That is ridiculous, it is past history. I haven't seen her for years.'

'Of course it is ridiculous,' Lalia agreed, surprised at the sense of relief that swept her. 'I—hinted at such a thing, but I fear she may not have cared for it.'

He startled her by flinging back his head with a shout of laughter.

'What an entrancing picture of a polite afternoon call! Two charming women clawing delicately at each other! Tiny tufts of hair floating in the air! Pay no heed to Edwina's kitten-scratches, my dear, she is, and always was, a mischievous imp.' He turned to go, still chuckling, but she put out her hand.

'Wait, Romey. I rode down to the sea yesterday morning with Malcolm Overton, Violet was—was unable to come with us. I thought later that perhaps I should not have gone.'

He raised his dark brows. 'I see no harm. Malcolm is no longer a callow youth goggling at you. I trust you enjoyed the ride.'

'Yes, I like Malcolm.' She paused, wondering whether to continue and was taken aback when she heard him ask,

'What else are you debating telling me? You've something else up your pretty sleeve, I know.'

'You seem to know a great deal too much about me,' she protested, half annoyed, half laughing. 'Well, Lady

Grenfell happened to see us riding and remarked on it in a way I did not like.'

'Oho! So that's it, she meant to make you think I would be jealous! But of course you know I would not.'

'Well, of course not, there is nothing whatever to be jealous about!'

'But if there *were* something,' he took a swift step towards her. 'You would not expect me to be jealous, would you, Lalia?'

She started to speak, then paused, suddenly aware of an uneasy undercurrent in his words.

'That fool of a Frenchman,' he said, 'I took you away from London because I did not intend you to become an object of scandalous gossip. Did you think, then, I was jealous because a man made love to you?'

'I—no, of course I did not,' she stammered, dismayed by something she glimpsed in his eyes. 'You were, perhaps rightly, angry with me . . . but not *jealous*.'

He looked at her for so long and so silently that she felt her heart begin to beat heavily and unevenly. He said abruptly, 'Of course I was not jealous; there is only jealousy when there is love.'

He left her to stare after him with quickened breath and a curious feeling of shock.

Mrs Brookford listened to Lalia's account of her call at Belmont and nodded and pursed her lips when Lalia confessed she had not liked Edwina Grenfell.

'I am afraid it is so with me; Edwina did not behave well . . . However, it is all past now and we must forget it. I do not suppose we shall see much of her.'

Some days later Lalia went with Romey to see how the work on the cottages was getting on, and to bring clothes and boots to some of the children. She was pleased to find herself at ease with him again after the curious little incident following her visit to Belmont. She spoke to the women, admired the babies and distributed sweets among the children. Roofs had been made rain-proof, floors boarded over, windows enlarged and land drained for gardens and fenced for livestock. The saw-mills were working once more, and the famous Dorset Horn sheep grazed on the smooth grassy hills, and the ploughed land was greening as she and Romey drove about the estate. She felt happy and carefree and Romey smiled down at her as he drove the dogcart team home.

'You must do this more often, it suits you, you have a fine colour.'

'Indeed, I would like to. But I am thinking of paying a short visit to Brighton, Romey. Aunt Flora is staying there and has expressed a wish to see me and I feel I ought to go. Kate is perfectly capable of caring for Elizabeth and your mother and Mrs Grant will manage the household. It is good to see your mother so bright and well isn't it?'

He nodded agreement. 'But she will need to repeat the treatment, probably in June or July. Her sister who has just returned from India is anxious to take her while she visits Doctor Helmer, she and mother have not met for some years.'

'Oh, she would enjoy that, I know. Then I shall arrange to visit Brighton next week.'

Minnie busied herself getting out trunk and valises and sorting clothes for packing. She was to accompany Lalia to Brighton, to her great delight. The journey was planned for Friday. Hotel rooms had been booked and train seats reserved. Lalia was in her room making out a list of shopping she intended to do in Brighton when Mrs Brookford sent for her.

She found her mother-in-law in her private sitting-room, looking pale and agitated.

'What is it?' Lalia asked anxiously. 'What has happened? Is Romey . . .'

'Oh dear! Such a shock for us! She is here, Mrs Carew,

Rosa's mother! She has come, she says, to take Elizabeth back to Spain with her!'

'But—she cannot do that!' Lalia cried.

'My dear, we must recognise she has more right to the child than we have. We cannot refuse Mrs Carew the right to care for her own grandchild.'

'But she refused to take her when I wrote.'

'Her circumstances are changed and she is now able to raise the child in a proper manner, she says. Dear Lalia, I know how great a shock this is to you, but I greatly fear we shall have to let little Elizabeth go!'

CHAPTER
SIXTEEN

Mrs Carew rose in a flutter of agitation as Lalia entered the room.

'Dear Mrs Brookford, I am glad I meet you! You have been most kind and good to my poor Rosa and my grandchild. I am so grateful to you and your husband. When you write, I am in distress that I cannot take the little baby because I have no money and my daughter hopes to marry a good man who would not like to know how Rosa has behaved to shame her family. So I must say no, but my heart is sad, you understand? Now, all is changed! My daughter is married!'

She paused for breath while Lalia looked at the small, plump woman whose sparkling dark eyes were so like Rosa's. This was the woman who wanted to take Elizabeth from her. She said, choosing her words carefully,

'I am glad your daughter is safely married, Mrs Carew, but I do not see how you could give Rosa's child a good life if, as you say, you are badly off. It is expensive to rear a child.'

'But I tell you, all is changed!' Mrs Carew's plump hands gesticulated frantically. 'I get money! Some person of my husband's family dies and I will have the money from him! It is not a very big money, but I can live nicely now and I can make a fine home for my granddaughter.'

'I . . . see.' Lalia's heart sank as she saw the joy in Mrs Carew's face. 'Well, this cannot be decided in too great a haste. Elizabeth is doing very well with us, she was premature, you know.'

'Ah, my poor Rosa. Always so quick . . . like a bird. She must always have her own way. The man, the child's father . . . he does not want her, I see that. I take Elizabeth now, please. I stay with a friend in London who does all the business for me. Then I return to Spain.'

'Oh no, you cannot snatch her away like that! We took her when no one wanted her,' Lalia cried. 'We have grown fond of her.'

'But I too love her! I weep much for my Rosa and think always of her little one. I am her grandmother and she is mine, Mrs Brookford! You are no relation, you have no claim, the child is not of your father. She will have good care and much love from me, I promise you.'

'I—I must speak to my husband,' Lalia faltered. 'This cannot be done in a hurry.'

'But yes, I must hurry! I do not like England so much, I wish to return to Spain with the baby.'

'Please sit down, Mrs Carew. Let me offer you some refreshment.' Glad of something to do that would give her time to collect her thoughts, Lalia pulled the bell-rope and instructed the footman to bring coffee and cake. As the man left the room, Romey entered. He was in riding clothes and his thick dark hair was ruffled and his coat and breeches mud-spattered.

'I took a toss, Blackie was in a bad mood . . .' he paused, seeing the visitor for the first time. His eyes went enquiringly to Lalia who hastened to introduce him.

'Mrs Carew has come, she says, to take Elizabeth to Spain with her,' she told him, conscious of the agitation in her voice. 'She . . . she has come into an inheritance and says she can now support Rosa's daughter. She wants to take Elizabeth from us, Romey.'

Mrs Carew burst into a flood of explanation. Romey listened, his brows drawn over intent eyes. When the flood had subsided, he turned to Lalia.

'She has a right to the child. We are no blood relations and Alvin will never claim her.'

'You mean . . . she can take Elizabeth away?' Lalia stared at him. 'But she is doing so well with us; we have grown attached to her. How do you *know* Mrs Carew has this money or is the right person to look after Elizabeth?'

'I shall make all necessary enquiries,' he said quietly, coming to her side, 'but I think you must resign yourself to losing Elizabeth, my dear. Mrs Carew would not have come if she was not sure of her rights and her ability to care for her grandchild.'

'I will love the little one,' Mrs Carew said softly and tears suddenly clouded her dark eyes. 'If I have the child, I shall feel not so sad at losing my Rosa.'

Lalia turned to pour out coffee and to disguise the tears that had risen unbidden to her own eyes. To lose Elizabeth, not to be able to watch her progress and rejoice in her increasing health and liveliness, to have empty rooms where there was now a nursery . . . For the first time she realised how much the child meant to her and she wondered if Romey had anything of the same sense of loss.

She provided their guest with coffee and cake and Romey, sitting beside her, began to talk quietly. Mrs Carey listened, sometimes nodding her head and at other times expostulating vehemently.

Lalia ceased to listen. She rose and went to the window and looked out at the bright day that seemed to mock her mood. Elizabeth would leave a gap in her life if she went away; how was she to fill it?

Mrs Carew departed, having agreed to come for Elizabeth in a week's time, and refusing to leave it longer. When Romey came back from seeing her into the hired carriage that had brought her from Dorchester, he came to Lalia and put an arm around her shoulder.

'I'm going up to London straight away to make sure she

has this inheritance, but that is all we can do. She is right, we have no claim, and the child will comfort her for the loss of Rosa. And perhaps it may be the best thing for Elizabeth to be with her own people.'

'I . . . shall miss her.' Lalia did not look at him.

His arm tightened around her. 'I know, I shall also. It is a disappointment for both of us. But it was not unexpected; Spanish family love is very strong and I guessed Rosa's mother would want the child and take her if ever she was in the position to do so.'

Lalia let herself lean against him, feeling comfort in the hard strength of his body and the clasp of his arm around her. They stood silent for some minutes and slowly her first dismay left her.

'I shall have to find something to stop my thinking about it,' she murmured. 'I feel . . . sad, Romey.'

'Of course you do. But your visit to Brighton—'

'Oh, I cannot go now!'

'You will go as arranged, my dear,' the firmness in his voice silenced her protest, 'and stay until I tell you to return. I go to London today and return tomorrow evening, and you will travel to Brighton on Friday as arranged.'

So he knew she was dreading the actual moment of Elizabeth's leaving. Impulsively she said, 'You are good to me, Romey, and I do appreciate your kindness and thoughtfulness.'

He released her abruptly, startling her. 'Did you expect me to be unkind and thoughtless?'

'No, of course not,' she said, confused by the sudden change in his voice and face. 'We have always been good friends.'

'Good friends,' he said slowly, 'yes, that was part of the bargain, wasn't it? Nothing more than friendship, ever.' He turned away. 'Pray excuse me, I have to make some arrangements before I leave.'

The day passed slowly and unhappily for Lalia. In her heart she knew Romey was right and she was prepared for his return next day with the information that Mrs Carew was indeed in a position to care for her grandchild and she was to take Elizabeth after Lalia had left for Brighton.

The moment of leave-taking was swift. Romey took her arm and drew her out of the nursery before the tears came. She was silent on the drive to Dorchester, fighting the desolation that seized her. As she bade Romey goodbye, a man came running up, followed by a porter with luggage.

Romey raised an arm. 'Overton! Good, you can look after my wife. Quick, man, the train's just off!'

Lalia turned from waving to Romey to see Malcolm entering the carriage.

He sank, panting, into the seat opposite her and pulled off his hat and gloves.

'That was a near thing, Mrs Brookford! Mother kept me back with messages for Fanny who is staying in Brighton.'

'And are you being sent to bring her back?' Lalia asked, smiling. Malcolm's company would keep at least some of her sorrow at bay for a time; Romey had known that when he hailed Malcolm.

As if he divined her mood, Malcolm set himself to amuse and entertain her and she was grateful to him, and for his swift sympathy when she told him she must lose little Elizabeth. He did not say much, but his look was eloquent. They parted on arriving at Brighton and he told her he and Fanny would call upon her.

Minnie was hanging up dresses and arranging the pretty silver-backed brushes and crystal scent bottles on the hotel dressing-table when a page delivered a great sheaf of deep red roses. The card with it made Lalia smile and sigh. She would have to scold Malcolm for being so extravagant, but it *was* charming of him.

She called upon her aunt next day and was received with tearful joy and enquiries about the tragedy of Rosa.

'Such a *dreadful* end,' Miss Flora sighed, 'but she was not a good woman, my dear. I hold her responsible for your dear father's death, and her conduct has perfectly ruined poor Mrs Prior's life. She writes to Alvin but he does not answer and she does not know how he is getting on in Jamaica.'

Lalia did not think it necessary to reveal the life Alvin was leading on the sugar plantation. She told her aunt of Mrs Carew's arrival and her claim upon Rosa's child.

'Oh, of course she has the prior claim,' her aunt said. 'I am sorry if you will miss the little one, but—' she coughed delicately and averted her eyes, '—you will probably—er—have a family of your own one day, my dear.'

Lalia rose abruptly. 'I shall call tomorrow, Aunt Flora, and take you for a walk by the sea.'

Malcolm was waiting when she returned to the hotel.

'Would you care to stroll along the front, Mrs Brookford? It is such a splendid day.'

Lalia glanced out of the window. The sea was an almost Mediterranean blue, reflecting the cloudless sky. Visitors were walking to and fro along the sea front, the women's pretty light-coloured dresses and bright parasols making gay patches of colour. There was a pleasant feeling of light-hearted gaiety in the air and it made Lalia say: 'Yes, I should like to.'

He kept her amused by pointing out celebrities on holiday from London and two foreign royalties who had suffered reverses of fortune in their respective countries. Later, they had tea in a café.

'It's marvellous luck your being here,' he exclaimed boyishly. 'I wish I need not leave so soon, but Mama wants Fanny back. The silly girl is by way of falling in love with some poet fellow she's met. Fanny can never do anything in moderation.'

There was no mistaking the admiration in his eyes as he sat opposite her at the little table. Lalia knew she was looking well in her white poplin with its frivolous little blue ruffles and her Italian straw hat wreathed in forget-me-nots and rosebuds. She invited him to bring Fanny to tea next day.

'It may take her mind off her poet for an hour,' she said mischievously.

A few days later she received a letter from her mother-in-law, who told her that Mrs Carew had taken Elizabeth and there was no doubt she would be loved and cared for. There was a little news about neighbours, and the cook's success with strawberry jam. The last sentence in the letter caught Lalia's attention.

'When do you plan to return? Forgive me if I say it might be a good idea for you to come soon. Lady Grenfell calls upon us often, and summons Romey to Belmont on the most flimsy of pretexts. He is there too often for my liking.'

Lalia put the letter down thoughtfully. Her mother-in-law disliked Edwina and for that reason would see all sorts of sinister meanings in her behaviour. It was ridiculous to think any attempt on Edwina's part to breath fire into the dead embers of Romey's affections could succeed. All the same, Edwina *was* a very beautiful and seductive woman, and an unscrupulous one, Lalia suspected. She had been piqued to discover Romey had so far forgotten her as to marry. If she truly did intend to make mischief . . .'

'I think I shall return home,' Lalia thought. 'It is not that I am disturbed by Edwina's behaviour, but I must at some time get used to the house without Elizabeth.'

She wrote to Romey that night telling him she intended to return in two days.

Next day Malcolm brought Fanny to call and from a certain restraint in their manner Lalia guessed Malcolm had been insisting on his sister's return home and Fanny, no doubt with the poet in mind, had been resisting. When Lalia mentioned her imminent return to Dorset she saw the quick, irritated glance Malcolm gave his sister as he said, 'We shall be returning also. Perhaps we might travel together, Mrs Brookford?'

'I've said I won't go till the week is out!' Fanny snapped.

Lalia hastily changed the conversation. She was not sure if she wanted Malcolm's company on the journey; with a sulky Fanny in tow, it might not be pleasant. She knew he was angry and could not help feeling slightly sorry for the scolding Fanny would get on the way back.

She spent most of the rest of her stay with her aunt and bade her goodbye the evening before she left for Dorset.

As her train drew near Dorchester, Lalia felt a little glow of pleasure at the thought of being in her own home again. She would miss Elizabeth, but the knowledge that she would be loved and treasured was a comfort and in time she would see it was all for the best.

She was eagerly looking out of the window as the train came into the station and felt her heart jump most unaccountably as a man's figure broke from the crowd and strode towards her.

'Romey!' she called, and opening the door she stepped out to meet him.

For a second she had the strange feeling he would take her in his arms and her breath caught in her throat. Then he was gripping her hands and smiling down at her.

'So Brighton lost its charm? I'm glad. The house has been a poor place without you.' He took her arm, leaving Minnie to deal with porters and luggage.

When the carriage was well clear of the town, Lalia asked,

'Is there any news? Has anything happened while I have been away?'

Something in his face made her lay her hand on his arm

and say quickly. 'Something *has* happened. Tell me, please.'

'Alvin has died.' He put his hand over hers, his eyes searching her face. 'It was a recurrence of the fever and he was not strong enough to fight it. I'm sorry.'

For a moment she was too shocked and saddened to speak. At last she said, 'It is . . . not so very unexpected I suppose. The life he has been leading . . .'

'I confess I was prepared for something like this. But what I was *not* prepared for was to find he has left the estate, Silverstone, to *me*!'

CHAPTER
SEVENTEEN

LALIA looked at him in amazement. 'Left it to *you*? But why?'

Romey shrugged. 'I'm in the dark as much as you. He thought me a dull dog, and I thought him . . . Well, the temptation to be selfish and to yield to passing desires can be largely blamed upon his upbringing.'

Lalia turned her head to look out of the carriage window. 'You once said something of the same to me.'

'*No!*' The vehemence in his voice startled her. 'You were spoiled by your father and aunt, yes, but you have a strength of character Alvin never had. I am sorry he has died—and I do not want his plantation.'

'Was it his to give? I mean, was it wrong of him to leave it to you when it should rightly belong to his family?'

'It was his. His father bought and developed Silverstone and left it in his will to Alvin.'

'Then you must keep it, Romey; Alvin wished you to have it.' She sighed. 'I must write to his mother, although she probably blames me for Alvin's elopement and death by now. I can understand her wish to blind herself to his failings, poor woman.'

They sat in silence, each occupied with unhappy memories and pity for the man whose bright promise had ended so poignantly.

Lalia found Mrs Brookford busy with preparations for her visit to London. She, too, had been saddened by the news of Alvin's death.

'Such a shock for his poor mother, she nursed hopes of

his returning one day, I know. It is good to have you back, my dear. I am sorry I must leave you so soon.'

'But I am glad you are to stay with your sister while you see Doctor Helmer again,' Lalia told her. 'We shall miss you, but I know how dear your sister is to you.'

Lalia was grateful for having the bustle of her mother-in-law's departure to occupy her thoughts for her first few days back at Hildon Manor. Thought of the early days of her engagement to Alvin saddened the hours when she was alone. He had destroyed himself, as Rosa had done; their bright spark had lasted so little a time.

Romey came upon her strolling thoughtfully in the birch grove and taking her arm, asked abruptly, 'You're thinking of Alvin, aren't you?'

'Yes, Alvin and Rosa, their lives ended so tragically.'

'Alvin brought you sorrow and for that I find it hard to forgive him. Yet if he had not jilted you . . .' he caught her shoulders and she felt his fingers grip her through the thin silk. 'Have you ever regretted marrying me? Tell me the truth.'

His voice, and a grimness about his mouth, made her draw back quickly.

'No—no, of course not. I am very happy here. You are good to me and I have everything I want.' But even as she said it, she knew it was not completely true. She had much, but not everything. There were times when she knew a restless longing—for what? She did not know.

He released her slowly and they resumed their walk. Suddenly Lalia saw a smart little phaeton bowling up the avenue.

'Someone is calling on us,' she exclaimed. 'I wonder who it is.'

'It is Edwina—Lady Grenfell, she likes to drive the phaeton herself; she's an excellent whip.'

'I must hurry back then.' Lalia gathered her skirts up and turned to retrace her steps. So this was one of

Edwina's visits which had so displeased Mrs Brookford.

Edwina was all in green, a colour that emphasised the shade of her eyes and made a striking contrast to her coppery hair.

'I heard you had returned,' she said as Lalia greeted her, 'so of course I had to welcome you back to Hildon Manor. Your mother-in-law must have missed you and is glad to have you back, I expect.'

A tiny spark lit in Lalia's eyes as she sat down on the sofa beside her guest.

'Romey missed me also,' she said, 'and he, too, is glad to have me back.'

'Of course,' Edwina tilted her head thoughtfully. 'But he has been so busy that . . . I have done my poor best to keep him from becoming *too* desolated. He has been excessively kind in advising me on some business matters which my poor female mind cannot grasp. I have protested at his spending so much time on my affairs, but he *will* persist in doing it!' She sighed, and then, as if struck by a sudden thought, said: 'Do you know, I have just discovered you are acquainted with Monsieur Voizard. We met him first in London and my husband liked him greatly. Such a cultured mind and such impeccable manners—but alas! such a naughty reputation!'

'Yes, I met Monsieur Voizard in London and at the Overtons,' Lalia said coldly. 'He is an interesting man.'

'I believe he professed a great admiration for you. I am afraid for such a man to single you out . . . But it is not, perhaps, my place to warn you.'

'No, it is not!' Lalia's eyes suddenly blazed. 'I must deplore your love of gossip, Lady Grenfell, and your insinuations about Monsieur Voizard. I do not wish to be impolite, but has it anything to do with you?'

'Oh dear, now I have offended you!' Edwina's slim hands fluttered out in a gesture of pleading. 'Romey is quite right, I am much too outspoken. I only wished to drop a hint because you are young and have not had my experience of society. I know how cruelly the world can censure the slightest, most innocent, deviation from the rules—the rules we must all obey if our reputations are not to suffer.'

'I assure you my reputation is in no danger—' Lalia began, then she paused as Romey came into the room.

He greeted Edwina and turned to Lalia to say: 'I've ordered tea to be set on the terrace now it is cooler.'

'Ah, delightful!' Edwina smiled up into his eyes. 'Romey knows how I delight in being out of doors.'

Lalia was silent, biting back the furious words that rose to her lips. Edwina was deliberately baiting her and she would not give her the satisfaction of showing her anger. What was her object in seeking to attach Romey to her? Was it sheer mischief because she was bored with country life? Or did it go deeper, a deliberate attempt to drive a wedge between Romey and his wife?

While she dispensed tea Lalia watched Edwina and saw, with growing anger, how seemingly careless references to the past, accompanied with soft laughter and confidentially lowered voice, set her and Romey apart. If he turned to speak to Lalia, Edwina drew him back with a touch on his arm and murmured: 'Oh Romey, *do* you recall—' Lalia found herself answering Romey shortly when he spoke, and pretending interest in throwing crumbs to a robin who was hopping hopefully near by.

Suddenly she could contain her disgust no longer and she rose, saying, 'Pray excuse me, Lady Grenfell. I must help Mrs Brookford with preparations for her visit to London.'

Edwina smiled sweetly. 'Of course I will, Romey will look after me. It will be like old times.'

Inside the house, Lalia paused with clenched hands and hot cheeks. How dare Edwina behave so shamelessly! A growing suspicion had become a certainty; Edwina

intended to regain her hold over Romey. She had
rejected him in favour of money and social position, and
now she had these she wanted Romey as well. Surely
Romey must see what was in her mind? But Edwina was
clever, and a man's vanity could be flattered by knowing a
beautiful woman found him attractive—and wanted him.

Mrs Brookford met her with an expressive glance. 'So
she is here again? Lalia my dear, Edwina is a dangerous
woman and I must warn you to be careful.'

'Might it not be as well to warn Romey too?' Lalia
asked.

'My dear, men are so blind! They will not realise . . .
However, now you are returned she will not have the
effrontery to call on such feeble pretexts.'

When Lalia returned to the drawing-room she found it
empty. Looking out of the window she saw the phaeton
disappearing down the drive accompanied by Romey
riding Blackie.

When she came down to dinner that night, Romey had
just come in and he apologised for being too late to change
out of his riding clothes. Lalia kept up a pretence of
conversation during the meal, but when they were alone
in the drawing-room she asked sarcastically what particu-
lar problem of house or business Edwina had invented to
persuade him to return with her to Belmont.

Romey's silence, which she interpreted as not
considering her question worth an answer, drove her into
a strange, hurtful recklessness.

'Do you not see she is simply making use of you?'

'She wanted my advice on some additions to her
London house which she wishes to make.'

'Then she should employ an architect, she is wealthy
enough. *I* do not mind her taking up so much of your time,
but possibly other people might consider it—strange.'

'Strange that I help a friend with her problems?'

'Strange that you are at the beck and call of a woman

who threw you over for an elderly, wealthy man!' Lalia flung at him, and felt her anger crumble at the cold contempt in his eyes before he rose and left the room.

The morning mail brought Lalia a letter from one of her few friends in Yorkshire. At the end of the letter the writer asked if Lalia knew that her cousin, Nina Grange, was staying in Dorchester with her grandmother. 'Lady Grange has taken Harriet on a round of country house-parties. I feel sorry for Nina, life with her grandmother cannot be very exciting for her.'

Lalia was about to make some comment on the news, but a swift glance at Romey held her silent. He was reading a newspaper, something he seldom did at break-fast, and showed no sign of being aware of her. Although the morning was warm, she suddenly felt cold, as if a chill wind blew upon her as she sat with the coffee pot before her. So he had not forgiven her for her angry outburst against Edwina. Perhaps she should not have spoken as she had last night, but then he ought not to obey Edwina's demands on his time.

She looked at the letter again and thought that indeed Nina would not find life gay with her grandmother.

'I feel quite sorry for her,' she thought, folding the letter. 'I used to find her boring and silly, but I realise now her life was dull with Aunt Mildred and her spiteful little sister. I *could* ask her to visit me.'

She looked up to see Romey putting away his paper and getting to his feet.

'I've decided I shall go to London with my mother,' he said. 'There is business to be seen to over this Jamaican estate. You do not mind being alone, do you?'

'Of course not.' She spoke with an indifference she was far from feeling. Was this to punish her? Did he truly have to go? Pride came to her aid and she said casually, 'I plan to invite Nina Grange to stay a few days, she is visiting her grandmother in Dorchester and it must be dull for her.'

He raised his eyebrows, but all he said was: 'As you like.'

When Romey and his mother had left, Lalia ordered the phaeton and set off for Dorchester. The weather had been dry, but now there was a feeling of change. Clouds lay strung along the horizon and a cool wind stirred the dusty hedgerows.

Nina's grandmother was not receiving visitors, but Nina, greatly astonished, ushered Lalia into a small stuffy room too full of furniture, and offered her coffee.

'I have come to ask if you would care to spend a few days at Hildon Manor,' Lalia told her. 'I have only just heard you were in Dorchester.'

'Oh, I did not think to tell you because . . .' Nina stopped, going pink.

'Because I was not perhaps very kind to you in Yorkshire,' Lalia ended the sentence for her. 'I am sorry, Nina. I would like it if you would spare me a few days. My husband and mother-in-law are away and I would like to have your company.'

Nina's surprise was unflattering, but her gratification was evident as she stammered, 'Oh, I should like it of all things! Grandmama is very strict, I may not go out alone, and she rests most of the day. I should greatly like to stay with you, Cousin Lalia.'

'Then I shall send the carriage for you the day after tomorrow,' Lalia said smiling. 'Is it necessary for me to ask your grandmother's permission?'

'Oh no, she will know who you are,' Nina assured her eagerly, and added in a burst of frankness: 'I think she will be quite glad to be rid of me; she didn't *want* to have me, you know.'

Something in the girl's face made Lalia say quickly: 'Well, I do want you and I look forward to seeing you in Hildon Manor.'

As she drove back, she wondered if she had invited

Nina because she disliked the idea of being alone and having too much time to think about losing Elizabeth and Edwina's behaviour and Romey's coldness, or if she had been genuinely moved to a charitable action.

'I'm afraid it is the former,' she thought sadly, 'I am too selfish to do otherwise. Romey is right, I think only of myself.'

But that was better than to keep thinking of Romey, of the coldness in his face and his unfriendly eyes and lack of warmth in his manner. They had not quarrelled; it would have been better if they had, because a quarrel would not have left undercurrents and unanswered questions and a feeling that something dark and threatening had come to blot out the sunshine. She shivered suddenly and drew her scarf around her shoulders. Life had changed and become uneasy with doubts.

'It is since Edwina came,' she thought bleakly. 'She wants to get Romey back. I believe she still loves him. But does he love her?'

CHAPTER
EIGHTEEN

On returning home, Lalia found the Overton family had called and she persuaded them to stay for tea.

'I am thankful Fanny is home,' Mrs Overton murmured. 'She stayed with my sister who was not, I consider, careful enough about the young people she invited to her house.'

'It is lovely to have you back with us,' Violet declared. 'We have been quite dreary without you and with Malcolm away too. We must take up riding again.'

Conversation was interrupted by the arrival of some other guests and more tea was ordered. Lalia was busy at the tea table when Malcolm came up.

'I think Fanny is getting over her poet fellow,' he told her. 'She is pretty subdued and is taking an interest in missionary work.'

'But *not* the curate, I hope?' Lalia said, laughing up at him.

'I hope not. Did you know he's been left quite a respectable income by an aunt?'

'Oh dear, then he can propose to Fanny!'

'Good heavens, no! He never showed any preference for Fanny, it was the other way about. Will you come riding with me soon?'

She refused, explaining she had a cousin coming to visit her.

Any fears Lalia might have had about the wisdom of inviting Nina soon vanished. Away from her domineering mother and peevish sister, Nina proved a pleasant if

uninspiring visitor and her gratitude when she realised
Lalia did not intend to parade her affluence and married
status became slightly embarrassing.

'I have never really *known* you, Cousin Lalia,' she
confided. 'You always seemed to be . . .' she hesitated,
then went on with a rush, 'so aloof. I had the notion you
despised us because we weren't pretty or well-dressed.'

'And you probably despised me for being so unfriendly,' Lalia said lightly, to hide the pang of guilt she felt. 'Let
us forget what we once thought of each other, shall we? I
have an invitation for us both to a croquet party at the
Vicarage on Friday. Let us hope the weather will be fine
for it.'

'Oh, that will be delightful! At home, Canon Cranton
will not allow it to be played at his parties, he disapproves
of it.'

'Cranton? That is the name of our curate?'

'Is it? How surprising. Perhaps he is a relation.'

'You can ask him on Friday.'

The dry September days had turned to grey skies and
occasional rain showers, but by Wednesday the sun had
returned and Nina, in a flutter of excitement, consulted
Lalia about her dress for the Vicarage party.

'I do not have anything new or very pretty,' she
confessed. 'Mama had to spend the money on clothes for
Harriet. But my blue poplin is quite smart, I think. It was
made from one of Mama's dresses and I have added some
lace to bring it into fashion.'

Lalia's doubts were confirmed when the dress was
displayed. It was badly made and the vivid colour was
unbecoming to Nina and a profusion of cheap lace
removed any charm the dress may have once had.

'It is very nice,' she said untruthfully, 'but I feel a softer,
warmer colour would suit you better.'

'Alas, I have nothing else,' Nina sighed.

'I have a dress I seldom wear, it is a pretty rose-pink

muslin. Would you agree to accept it as a present, Nina?
Or would you think me horribly patronising?'

'Oh *no*! Dear Lalia, how excessively kind of you! You
have such beautiful taste. I have always admired your
lovely gowns, they made ours look quite horrid.'

Once again guilt swept Lalia and she said hastily: 'I'm
sure you always looked very nice. Let us try the rose
muslin, luckily we are much the same size.'

There were a few alterations to be made and Minnie
was set to work. When Friday came, Lalia surveyed her
cousin with satisfaction and some of her guilt left her. In
rose muslin, her hair arranged becomingly and topped
with a flower-trimmed hat—also Lalia's—Nina, her
cheeks flushed with excitement, was very near prettiness.

The Overtons had already arrived at the Vicarage
when Lalia and Nina drove up. Malcolm joined Lalia as
she stood watching the croquet players and asked if she
were not joining them. When she shook her head, he
asked when she would ride with him again.

'I really cannot say. After my cousin leaves, Romey
returns and I shall probably be busy.' Something in his
expression made her turn away, but he put his hand on her
arm, restraining her as he said in a low voice,

'I never see you alone now. I must speak to you, I
cannot go on meeting you only in my dreams!'

There was no mistaking the ardour in his voice and
face. Lalia was about to speak when she heard a cool,
slightly husky voice behind her drawl, 'Why, I do believe
naughty Malcolm is trying to persuade you to ride out
with him now Romey is neglecting you by rushing off to
London.'

Lalia jerked her arm free of Malcolm's hand. Edwina's
eyes were amused—and far too perceptive. Angry with
Malcolm, and with herself, she said coldly,

'I have no time to ride, I have a guest staying. Malcolm,
do you see my cousin? I expect she would like some tea.'

'Mr Cranton has just taken her in to have tea,' Malcolm replied. 'But may I take you into the house for some, Mrs Brookford?'

'No, thank you, I shall take tea later.' Lalia moved away, her head high and her lips tight. How unfortunate that Edwina should have appeared at just that moment! Probably she had heard Malcolm's most injudicious words. Really, she must scold him for showing his admiration so openly. Only, *was* it just admiration, or was he falling in love with her? Should she—*could* she—check him? She was honest enough to admit his love would not shock her as it ought to. Was it the answer to the strange hunger she sometimes felt? She had done with love, of course; yet to know she was loved by Malcolm would be very sweet comfort.

Nina's face was bright with excitement when they drove home.

'Was it not strange? Mr Cranton is our Canon's nephew. I was quite amazed. We had a long talk, for he wished for news of his uncle and I could tell him about the poor Canon's gout and his new housekeeper.'

'And Adolphus Cranton took you in to tea and played croquet with you and escorted you, alone, around the garden,' Lalia said, laughing. 'Did you enjoy it all?'

'Oh yes!' Nina sighed ecstatically. 'And Mr Cranton has asked if he may call at Grandmama's. Do you think she will object?'

Lalia stopped herself in time from saying: 'Not if she has any sense; you will make an excellent curate's wife,' and said instead, 'I am sure she will allow your Canon's nephew to call. When I write and thank her for letting you visit me I shall mention Mr Cranton's excellent character and highly moral behaviour—and that he has a comfortable income and will no doubt rise rapidly in his profession.'

Nina thanked her rapturously and went into a day-

dream obviously concerned with the highly moral
Adolphus and was returned to her grandmother next day
still in this happy state.

Mrs Brookford wrote to say her treatment had again
helped her condition and she was accepting her sister's
invitation to stay with her in Suffolk for a month. Romey
approved of this plan. He asked her to say he might not be
returning yet awhile.

Lalia was sitting on the terrace, enjoying the mellow
September sunlight, while she read the letter. She let it
fall and leaned her chin on her hand as she gazed across
the dewy lawns to distant fields and woods veiled in a faint
blue haze.

So Romey was still angry with her, so angry that he
would not write to her himself to say his business must
keep him in London longer. And this because she had
criticised Edwina's behaviour and expressed perfectly
reasonable resentment with it. It was not possible that
Romey could be unaware of Edwina's designs.

'I am his wife,' she thought, 'he should protect me from
her mischief-making. He *must* know she dislikes me! She
tries to ignore me when he is here, to shut me out. It is
abominable! I will not be frightened by her veiled threats
about Claude Voizard and Malcolm and if Romey listens
to her wicked insinuations, he is very wrong! I am his
wife.'

Yes, his wife . . . and yet, not his wife. She rose
restlessly and began to pace the terrace, the skirts of her
blue dress sweeping the warmed flagstones. Why had she
been so uneasy recently, so restless, almost appre-
hensive, as if some disaster threatened her? Even Nina's
visit had not chased away a shadow that drew ever nearer.
And this strange craving in her heart for something,
something missing in her life; what did it mean and why
would it give her no rest?

Suddenly the longing rose in a great wave and engulfed

her, making her throat ache with unshed tears and tearing at her heart. She was standing, her hands clasped to her breast, staring unseeingly across the lawns, when Malcolm strode onto the terrace.

'What is it? You are pale and there are tears in your eyes!' He pulled her roughly to him. 'You are sad . . . Lalia my darling, I cannot bear it! You must not be sad, I won't let you!'

'Malcolm—let me go! You must not!' She tried to break free, but he held her too fiercely. She had never seen him like this, so stern and with his eyes so full of longing and his tone so passionate.

'No, I shall never let you go! You are mine, you always have been. *He* does not care, he leaves you alone to be sad and weep . . . I love you, Lalia! My whole life was nothing until I knew you, my most dearest darling!'

She ceased to resist. This was her hunger, to be loved, to be desired, to be a fire in a man's blood that gave him no peace! Recklessly she raised her face to meet his kisses, letting her senses drown in his passion.

'Lalia my darling . . . My own very dear one. I tried—God! how I tried to forget you, to break away from you—but I could not. You are my very heart, Lalia!'

'This is wrong, Malcolm,' she whispered, 'very wrong, but—do you truly love me?'

'My God, do you doubt it? Don't you know I've been through hell having to pretend? But to see you sad and with tears in your eyes . . . I can pretend no longer. Lalia, we must—'

'Hush!' She raised her head listening. 'I hear Simpson coming. I told him to see me about my mare, Betsy, she has gone lame. You must go, Malcolm, at once! Oh please—go. Now!'

He released her reluctantly and stood looking down at her flushed face with ardent eyes. 'Very well, but I shall return, my dearest Lalia. You know I shall, don't you?'

'Yes,' she whispered, stepping back, her hands going to her disordered hair, 'but I beg you to go now.'

.He hesitated, then as a heavy footfall sounded he turned and left the terrace and a few moments later she heard him ride away.

'Pardon, Ma'am,' Simpson's rugged face appeared around the corner of the terrace, 'I didn't take trouble to come afore seeing Master's back and gives me orders 'bout Betsy.'

For a second the sky wheeled about Lalia's head and she caught at the balustrade to steady herself. 'The *master*?'

'Aye, he's seen to Betsy, like I said, Ma'am.' Simpson touched his cap and retreated.

Lalia's heart began to race wildly and the blood drummed in her ears as fear gripped her. He must not see her like this, with her hair disordered and her face flushed and burning from Malcolm's kisses. She turned hastily to the house—and saw Romey standing just inside the French windows!

CHAPTER
NINETEEN

In the silence that fell Lalia could hear the heavy drumbeat of her heart. She was suddenly as cold as ice as she met the eyes of her husband, the man she had married without love, who had found her in the arms of another man and seen her surrender to his passionate words of love and his kisses. She knew without asking that Romey had seen and heard everything, standing silently in the shadows and thinking . . . what? She tried to speak, but no words would come from her frozen lips. She could only stand, staring.

At last he spoke, his voice devoid of all emotion and as chill as his eyes.

'I appear to have arrived most inopportunely.'

'I . . .' desperately she tried to control the fit of trembling that shook her, making her voice weak. 'I did not know you intended to return so soon. Your mother said—'

'I changed my mind; my business was done.'

A suspicion lit a tiny flame of anger in her, warming her taut nerves.

'Did you come back to spy on me?'

She shrank from the blaze in his eyes.

'No. Oddly enough, I have always trusted you. I never took your flirtation with the Frenchman very seriously, but Malcolm . . . Is he your lover?'

'How dare you ask that!' Now she had the flame of her anger to release her from fear.

'I have every reason to think he is. I have been mistaken

in him, he hid his passion well for so young a man, but not from you, of course. You knew he loved you—and encouraged him.'

'I did not know!' She bit her lip. *Had* she known or had she only suspected? But she had never encouraged him, although to know he loved and longed for her had been an easing of the hunger in her heart. 'It was . . . the first time he declared his . . . his feelings for me.'

'And so you allowed him to take you in his arms, to kiss you and confess he had always loved you! You, my wife, to behave like this when I am away!' Suddenly his restraint broke and he strode to her and caught her shoulders in a grip that made her cry out in pain. 'How dare you behave so!'

She put her hands against his broad chest, thrusting him away furiously, her anger casting out all caution.

'And *you*, spending your time with Edwina Grenfell while *I* was away! Letting her cozen you, listening to her trying to lure you away, to recapture your love! But perhaps,' her voice grew bitter, 'she did not have to try very hard. You loved her once and perhaps being jilted merely increased your love! Perhaps *she* is *your* mistress!'

His hands fell away. 'You believe that?'

'Am I the only one? What do you imagine neighbours think when you are always at her beck and call? When she makes it plain she despises me and thinks me of no account? Your mother warned me she was dangerous!'

'My mother has always disliked her.'

'But it is quite evident you do not.'

'No, I don't dislike her.'

'You still love her?' When he did not answer, she moved back from him, shaken by an intensity of feeling that was like a knife stab.

'*Do you love Malcolm*? Answer me, Lalia! *Do you love him*?'

'*Yes!*' she flung at him. 'Yes—I do!' Frantically she

sought for words to hurt as she was hurt, to stab his heart in return for this tearing pain. 'What is it to you if I do? *You* do not want my love . . . You wanted only a Golden Bride!' Her words faltered before the flare of something hot and primitive in his eyes.

'So you *can* love,' he said softly. 'I thought you were done with love, my snow-maiden wife! You had no true love for Alvin, and none for me . . . But Malcolm's arms and kisses are sweet to you—as mine will never be!'

Before she knew his intention, he had pulled her roughly into his arms, crushing her slender body against his in a cruel grasp, and was kissing her with a harsh, fierce passion that made her senses swim. His hand was on her breast and his kisses, demanding, terrifying, awakening a tearing surge of feeling that answered him with passion as primitive as his! Her world shook and splintered around her. This was something she had never known, never guessed existed!

He released her so abruptly that she stumbled and almost fell. His eyes, burning darkly in his white face, rested on her for a breathless moment, then without a word he turned and left her.

She sank onto a chair, waiting for the blood to cease surging through her body in a hot tide, and trembling at the memory of the ecstasy his kisses had brought her, leaving her unable to think and powerless to put her shattered world together again.

How quiet it had grown; as if everything was holding its breath and was waiting . . . Then from the stables came the ring of hoofs on cobbles and Simpson's voice. Then silence again.

Lalia put a trembling hand to her forehead and found it burning. She had lied to Romey. She did not love Malcolm. His declared love had for a brief moment been a comfort, soothing her strange craving that had grown inside her and gave her no peace. She knew she had been wrong in accusing Romey of being Edwina's lover, but he was not blameless. He had said cruel things about her and Malcolm that had aroused a fierce desire to hurt him. He could not truly think she had been unfaithful and that she loved Malcolm. He, too, had been angry and had wanted to hurt her. She must make him see how wrong they had both been, but not now, not while she still trembled at the memory of his harsh embrace and her thoughts were in turmoil. She lay back, closing her eyes while she fought for composure.

She did not know how long she sat there. At last she heard steps and looked up to see Mrs Grant regarding her with a disturbed expression on her usually placid face.

'Mr Brookford asked me to give you this—after he had left.' She held out a letter, folded and sealed.

'He has left?' Lalia rose swiftly. 'But—he has only just arrived! When—when did he leave?'

'He's ridden off on Blackie, Miss Lalia dear, and Simpson is told to follow with the luggage.' Mrs Grant's eyes were troubled as she watched the colour leave Lalia's face. 'Is . . . is everything all right, Miss Lalia dear?'

Lalia pulled herself together with an effort. 'Oh . . . there is nothing the matter, Granty. Of course, I knew he had to return to London, although not quite so soon. He—he must have decided it was something important.' The words came out jerkily as her mind tried to take in Romey's abrupt departure. She waited until the housekeeper had left her and then tore the seal and read what Romey had written.

'I have decided to visit the Jamaican plantation Alvin left me. There is a steamship sailing from Bristol in two days time and with luck I shall board it. Apply to Ransome for any help you may need, he will deal with all financial problems. When I get the estate in good order, I shall sell it and can then repay you all you have put into the Hildon estate. Romey Brookford.'

He had left her! He had chosen to leave without any explanation, believing she loved another man! He had gone—perhaps for ever. It was cruel! Unfair! Wicked! But as she crushed the letter in her cold hands, a voice inside her whispered: 'You let him believe it. You told him you loved Malcolm.'

The sound of wheels made her heart leap. Simpson was driving the cart used for luggage down the avenue at a smart pace. She watched it with wide, frightened eyes until it was out of sight.

'I told him a lie,' she thought, and a knife-thrust of memory brought back the old gypsy's words: 'There's girt trouble for you . . . You will tell a lie—an' regret it wi' pain and tears!'

'I . . . don't want . . . him to go!' The words came out slowly as if, deep inside her, they had been waiting to be dragged into the light of truth. 'Romey—don't leave me! I lied! I—I want you to come back to me . . . *please*!'

'You will regret it wi' pain an' tears!'

The pain and tears had come, crushing her. But the tears lay too deep to be shed. They ached, as her heart ached. It was too late to weep, Romey had gone and he would never know what in a blinding flash of truth she knew at last, that she loved him and wanted him to love her as a true husband!

September died in a glory of rich colours and high, brilliantly blue skies and sharp sunlight, and October burst in to send the red and gold leaves scurrying before a blustery wind and to veil the morning and dusk in cool mists. The sun sank lower on its travels across the sky, as if bowing to the oncoming winter. In the garden and grounds of Hildon Manor, gardeners swept leaves from paths and lawns, tidied flower beds and tied up plants and lit bonfires whose sweet-smelling smoke drifted in

through the window of the morning-room where Lalia sa
writing to her Aunt Flora.

'Romey has had to visit his Jamaican sugar estate.
manage very well on my own—my mother-in-law is stil
with her sister in Suffolk—but I have been kept indoors by
a stupid chill which persists despite the doctor's ministra
tions. If you would care to visit me, Aunt Flora, you wil
be most welcome.'

She paused to look out of the window, resting her head
on her hands and wondering if the curious malaise tha
afflicted her was indeed the result of a chill, or if the shock
of Romey's departure had brought on the grey depression
and desire to avoid all society, even that of Viole
Overton who had called several times.

Malcolm had not come again. She had written to him
the night Romey had left, a letter that she knew mus
cruelly wound him, but which had to be written. News
reached her that he had gone abroad again. Well, it was
better so, he was young and ardent and nature would soon
heal his wound. She could think of him with kindness
threaded with bitterness. If only he had not sought he
that morning!

James was instructed to deny all callers, but even hi
vigilance was not proof against one visitor.

Lalia, wrapped in a warm cloak for the wind was chill
was strolling in her favourite birch grove when she saw a
figure approaching. She stiffened, recognising the rich
furs and flash of coppery hair under the elegant hat with it
bird's wings and ribbon bows. As she turned quickly
Edwina called out,

'Don't go, I must talk to you.'

Lalia waited for her to come near before saying: 'I have
told James to say I am not receiving visitors just now.'

'Oh, he told me, but I took no notice. I am not an
ordinary caller, you know. When I think of how long and
how well I have known Romey . . . I want to know why he

as gone to Jamaica. Surely there is some kind of overseer
o look after the estate? There was no need for Romey to
o rushing off like that.'

'I think that is for Romey to decide, Lady Grenfell.
ilverstone plantation has been neglected and needs
utting in order and Romey felt it his duty to find out the
onditions there.'

'He could have sent someone out, surely?' Edwina
ucked a copper curl under her hat. 'It seems exceedingly
dd to me. Of course, Jamaica is a very beautiful island,
Romey has often told me.' She smiled and Lalia,
ecognising the smile, instinctively braced herself. 'Do
ou know, he suggested *I* visited the island sometime
ince I am so fond of foreign travel. I wonder he did not
ake you with him.'

'I have no desire to see Jamaica,' Lalia said shortly.
Was that the reason you wished to talk to me?'

'I wanted news of Romey, and to know why he has gone
ff like this. I quite miss him, you know.'

'Naturally, since you are such an *old* friend.'

'Does he return soon? I have so many things I want to
iscuss with him, he is always such a great help to me. A
voman on her own—'

Lalia swung around to face her squarely. 'A woman on
er own would be wise not to meddle too much with
nother woman's husband, Lady Grenfell. I am sorry,
ut I must speak frankly, perhaps I should have done so
efore. Romey is my husband, and you are making your-
elf conspicuous by your striving to attach him to you.
'ou loved him once; am I to understand you do so still?'

She watched, unmoved, the green eyes blaze in a
uddenly pale face.

'I find you unforgivably rude and insulting,' Edwina
aid icily. 'You would like to forget Romey once loved
ne, but he has not forgotten. I do not have to *try* to get him
ack, he will come willingly. You cannot hold him! Do

you think I don't know why he married you? You
money—'

'Please go,' Lalia spoke softly, but something in he
voice and face made the other woman pause uncertainly
'*You* have been both rude and insulting and I shall no
forget it. I do not wish to see you again and you will not b
welcome at Hildon Manor.'

Edwina's laugh was shrill. 'But how surprising to fin
you are jealous, quite furiously jealous of me!' She turne
and walked swiftly back the way she had come.

Edwina was right, Lalia thought bleakly. Why had he
jealousy of Romey's one-time love not shown her wher
her heart lay? She knew now the strange longing, th
growing hunger, had been for Romey's love. He ha
kissed her in anger and would never know that his kiss ha
revealed the truth to her at last. He did not want her love
and she must love him silently for ever.

The tears she had not shed when Romey left her cam
suddenly and she leaned against one of the silvery birc
trunks and wept with an abandon and despair that left he
weak and empty of all emotion. When she finally returne
to the house, Mrs Grant, after a swift glance at he
stricken face, ordered her to bed as if she were still a chil
and stood over her while she tried to eat some of th
supper brought to her.

As she took away the tray of almost untouched food
Mrs Grant said abruptly, 'Why don't you go up to Londo
for a little trip, dearie? You're too lonely here, what wit
not wanting visitors, and now Mrs Brookford planning t
go to Italy with her sister for the winter. It isn't good fo
you to be so much alone—and I'd have said as much to M
Brookford if I'd known he was to go off to foreign part
like he has.' She ended with an indignant sniff and Lali
hastened to say,

'He had to go, Granty, the plantation is worth a lot o
money.' Money with which he would repay her, sh

thought unhappily. Soon he would have no need of her fortune, and no need of her. The thought made her turn her head so Mrs Grant should not see the tears filling her eyes.

'I'll bring you a milk drink so you'll sleep,' the housekeeper promised, and went off with a worried frown creasing her forehead.

'Perhaps she is right and I would be better in London, I would not be reminded . . . of everything,' she thought forlornly. 'It would be a change. And I would like to consult Mr Ransome about renting the water meadows, and buying more sheep.'

She did not sleep until the night began to fade, and then she slept heavily and did not wake until nearly noon. When she awoke, her mind was made up. She would go to London, taking Minnie, and would notify Mr Ransome she intended to call upon him the day after she arrived.

She travelled to London at the end of the week. This time she felt no pleasure, no excitement in the busy streets and crowds, no desire for entertainment. When she mounted the dusty stairs to Mr Ransome's office she had an oppression of spirits she could not banish.

She thought that the young clerk who ushered her into Mr Ransome's inner office looked at her oddly, but she brushed the thought aside and greeted the man who had risen to meet her.

'Good morning, Mr Ransome. I am glad you could see me, I have several problems I would like you to . . .' she broke off, aware of something frightening in the lawyer's usually composed face. 'Mr Ransome, is anything wrong?'

'Dear Mrs Brookford, let me get you a chair.' He brought it forward and waited for her to seat herself. 'I am afraid what I have to say will be a shock. Of course, we must not jump to conclusions and much may be exaggerated and events not quite so disastrous as—'

'Mr Ransome,' Lalia said sharply, a cold chill creeping up her spine, 'what are you trying to tell me? What has happened?'

He hesitated, looking at her from under his thick brows.

'I am sorry to have to tell you, Mrs Brookford, that we have just had news of a very severe hurricane in Jamaica following an earthquake.'

Lalia sat as if turned to stone, her mind for a second refusing to accept his words. 'An earthquake . . .'

'It was not one of their worst earthquakes, but the hurricane has caused much damage along the coast and also inland. And there is grave fear of cholera.'

'My husband's estate, Silverstone,' she forced her stiff lips to move, 'is it . . .?'

'I fear it was in the path of the hurricane, but we have no news yet of how much damage has been done. There is every hope your husband may have been in some place that did not suffer so badly. And the estate houses usually have storm cellars for such an event. In all probability we shall hear from him or get news of him soon.'

Lalia rose swiftly, pulling her fur cape around her.

'Mr Ransome, please discover immediately what vessel sails for Jamaica and get me a passage on it.'

'My dear Mrs Brookford, such a thing is impossible!' Mr Ransome's face was a study in horrified astonishment and dismay. 'You cannot go out to an island that has just been ravaged by—'

'I am going. If you will not find me a berth on some ship, I shall have to seek elsewhere.' Lalia met his shocked gaze with a firmness he recognised he could not break.

'Very well, but I most earnestly protest. I consider it to be *most* unwise, positively reckless, Mrs Brookford. I do beg you to reconsider.'

'I am sorry to distress you, Mr Ransome,' she said quietly, 'but my mind is made up. *I am going to Jamaica.*'

CHAPTER
TWENTY

'TRAVEL all the way out to Jamaica where there's earth-quakes and hurricanes and plague?' Mrs Grant's face was aghast with horror. ' 'Tis not to be thought of! The dangers—'

'If there are dangers, then I must face them,' Lalia met the housekeeper's eyes steadily. 'My husband is there, perhaps injured, perhaps sick. I must go to him.'

'But 'tis no place for a lady like yourself. I've heard tell of wild folk there and white folk being murdered. And—and you may be drowned! I've no trust in those steamships.' Tears began to trickle down Mrs Grant's face.

Lalia put her arms around her. 'Dear Granty, do not be afraid for me. Steamships are safe, and conditions on the island may not be as bad as we imagine.' She did not reveal that the Governor had declared a state of disaster. 'If my husband is ill, it is my duty to go to him. Granty, I *cannot* remain here, dreading news, not knowing how he is or . . . I must go to him, *now*!'

Mrs Grant looked at her and nodded slowly. 'Aye, dearie, I see you must. And my heart is sore for you. May God protect you and him.'

'He will, I know it. Now, you must help me, I must pack at once. I have a passage on the *Sea Queen* and must be in Bristol by Tuesday morning.'

'I'll not let you go alone, your dear mother left you in my charge.'

Lalia shook her head. 'Bless you, Granty, but I will

take no one. It is quite possible my husband is well and will meet me when I arrive. Pray do not be anxious, all will be well.'

Her words were brave, but in her heart there was a terrible fear that Romey might be hurt or ill—or perhaps dying! Perhaps—her heart seemed to die within her at the dreadful thought—already dead! The death toll was growing; two small villages had been swept into the sea with no survivors, and reports of houses razed to the ground, forests flattened and rivers breaking their banks made a picture that haunted her day and night.

Mr Ransome, protesting to the end, had procured her a passage on a ship taking grain, together with hastily assembled medical supplies, to the island.

Mrs Overton came to the house and swept Lalia into her arms.

'Oh my poor child! What terrible anxiety for you. Let us pray you will soon have news of your husband's safety. This waiting—'

'I shall not wait, Mrs Overton, I sail for Jamaica in two days.'

Mrs Overton's horror matched Mrs Grant's. In vain she begged Lalia to consider the conditions she might find on the estate, the risk of cholera, lack of all amenities and possible trouble with natives, but Lalia remained silent and at last her friend, seeing her words were having no effect, sighed and said,

'I see I cannot move you, my dear. Well, you go with my prayers for you and your husband's safety and I shall not be easy until I get news that all is well. If I thought my husband could persuade you . . .'

'Dear friend, no one can persuade me. I cannot remain here while Romey may be injured or ill.'

'You are a brave and most loving wife.' Mrs Overton kissed her and left, looking worried and unhappy.

A fever of impatience gripped Lalia and she could not

sit still but roamed the house restlessly. Mrs Grant had packed a case of medical supplies and another of non-perishable food and Lalia had herself packed a valise of Romey's clothes. If the plantation house had been destroyed all in it would be buried or ruined.

Mr Overton insisted on accompanying her on the train journey to Bristol. His deep disapproval and anxiety for her safety was evident, but he made no attempt to dissuade her. When he had seen her safely aboard the *Sea Queen* she clasped his hand in gratitude.

'Thank you, dear Mr Overton, for your kindness. I shall send news as soon as possible to relieve your anxiety. All may not be so bad as reported.'

He shook his head in sombre doubt and bade her farewell. She hastened down to her tiny cabin, shaken by a sudden realisation of what she had undertaken. If Romey was unhurt, how would he greet her arrival? What, if any, would be her welcome? He had left her because he thought her faithless, her love given to another man. How could she make him realise his mistake? And would he believe her when she told him she had lied?

'I shall *make* him believe me,' she thought as she sat on the narrow bunk, aware of the gentle movement of the ship beneath her. 'I shall tell him I love him and that I want his love. I had meant to hide my love, but I know I cannot! If he chooses Edwina . . .'

But he had left Edwina also, he had not gone to her when he left Hildon Manor. There was some comfort in the thought for Lalia's bruised heart and she clung to it. If he did not love Edwina, there might be a chance he would in time grow to love his wife. If only she could believe that!

The ship sailed with the tide. At supper, Lalia met the captain and other passengers as the ship swung down the channel and out to open sea. Captain Morris, a small, spare man with a quick eye and reserved manner, greeted her briefly and had no further news of conditions in Jamaica. The other passengers, a mother with two small children, two middle-aged business men and an elderly woman rejoining her husband, were silent after their first greeting, and it was obvious their collective thoughts were on the ravaged island of Jamaica.

Lalia slept heavily that night, worn out by the strain of the last days. In the morning she went on deck before breakfast, grateful for the fresh breeze after the stuffiness of her cabin. The elderly woman, a Mrs Jordan, joined her.

'Pray heaven we'll have a smooth journey,' she observed, inspecting the sparkling sea around them with a practised eye. 'I have crossed this sea six times and it has never behaved the same way twice.'

Lalia turned quickly. 'You live in Jamaica? Do you have news of how things are there now?'

'The earthquake was not serious I think, but the hurricane has done much damage,' Mrs Jordan told her, wrapping her shawl around her shoulders. 'I do not know what I shall find when I arrive.'

'Has there been—been much loss of life?'

'There is little news yet and one hopes for God's mercy.' Mrs Jordan looked at Lalia sharply. 'Are you visiting someone? It is a poor time to do so.'

'I am going out to my husband,' Lalia told her. 'His estate is Silverstone, a sugar plantation on the eastern coast. I—I am hoping it may have escaped the worst of the high winds.'

'Oh, you poor child!' Mrs Jordan exclaimed. 'What an anxiety for you. But many of the planters' houses are sturdy, with cellars for just such a disaster. Of course, the sugar fields will be wrecked, I fear, and the stupid workers will have fled as they always do when they are most needed.'

'Has there been any insurrection on the island lately?'

Lalia asked. 'Now there is no slavery, surely the people are content?'

Mrs Jordan's lips tightened for a moment before she said: 'There are always some malcontents who resent their white masters. On my husband's estate we have had a few . . . unpleasant evidences of this. The people are simple and easily led by a firebrand with crazy notions of throwing all the white people out and governing the island himself. Come, let us seek breakfast, this breeze has given me a fine appetite.'

The sea changed its mood and Lalia was forced to stay in her cabin, listening to the wind whine and feeling the ship dip and rise and shudder as the waves hit it. The mother of the two children became ill and, although not feeling well herself, Lalia took the children and told them stories and played games with them until the storm ceased and the pale-faced passengers could foregather on the deck again and strain their eyes searching the horizon.

Captain Morris took Lalia aside one morning and asked her how she planned to reach her husband's estate when they docked at St Anna's Bay and she had to confess she had no ideas as yet.

'Silverstone estate is a good way from St Anna's,' he said, looking worried, 'must be all of fifteen miles inland, and it's likely there'll be little left of roads and no kind of transport for a lady.'

'I can ride,' she told him. 'Can't I get a horse, or a mule? And perhaps someone to guide me.'

He looked dubious. 'Roads and trails could be washed away and rivers sometimes change course after a 'quake, and coloured folk don't like going into devastated areas, they're afraid of duppies.'

'Duppies?' she asked. 'What are they, please?'

'Kind o' ghosties, bad spirits the blacks believe in. Scares 'em badly. They believe duppies haunt places where there's been high winds. You won't catch no sugar workers around after a hurricane, they skitter for the hills and hide.'

'Well I shall find *someone* to guide me,' she said firmly.

'Mebbe you could bribe a poor white,' the Captain remarked, stroking his beard. 'If you can get away, I'll see your baggage is safe stored in the town for you.'

She thanked him and went to her cabin to make a list of such medicine and stores she could carry with her on horseback. Perhaps she might be lucky enough to hire a packhorse, then she could take more.

To her restless spirit the days seemed appallingly long and empty and she had too much time to think. What had Romey's true feelings been when he asked her to marry him? Had he wanted only her fortune, or had he as well a liking for her strong enough to make him content to share his life with her? They had got on well together; she had become interested in his work on the estate and she knew he appreciated it. He had been magnanimous over Rosa and her child, not every man would receive a child born out of wedlock into his home and she guessed he had done it for her. He had comforted her when little Elizabeth had been taken away.

She had incurred his anger only when he found her with Claude Voizard and when Malcolm had so unfortunately declared his love for her and she had sought to find comfort in his embrace. Romey had not been jealous or he would have challenged Malcolm—or beaten her. He believed she loved Malcolm, and had left her. She had indeed regretted her lie with pain and tears.

The weather continued calm and at first sight of a smudge on the horizon everyone's heart lifted.

'It will not be long now,' Mrs Jordan remarked, 'until we know the worst. St Anna has not been badly hit by the hurricane and I shall stay with friends there until I get news of my husband upcountry. Will you come with me, Mrs Brookford? I know my friends will welcome you.'

Lalia thanked her and explained her plan for riding to Silverstone without delay if she could find a horse and a guide.

'My friends can probably help,' Mrs Jordan said, 'they keep a stable and may be able to let you have a horse and a mule to carry the baggage. A guide may be more difficult.'

The sun was blinding and the heat oppressive as they docked in the little harbour of St Anna. Lalia accompanied Mrs Jordan, who had insisted she should spend the night with her friends before setting out for Silverstone. Although the small town had escaped the worst of the storm, Lalia saw many roofless houses and flattened fences, and debris of all kinds lay strewn about the town. Mrs Jordan's friends welcomed her warmly and promised her a horse and mule and sent around the town to find a man willing to be a guide.

When they were alone, Mrs Jordan said abruptly: 'It isn't good news about your husband's estate, my dear. Part of the river was diverted and has done damage and the workers and staff have fled to the hills and, as yet, there is no news of your husband and his overseer. The roads are washed away and you will have to ride over much rough country and perhaps have to return without reaching Silverstone.'

Lalia had turned pale at her first words, but now she straightened her slim shoulders, her face resolute.

'I shall not return; I am going to reach Silverstone, if I have to walk there, I shall do it!'

Unexpectedly, the old lady kissed her. 'You are a brave creature. I'd have done the same at your age. May God grant you find your man safe and sound.'

A mulatto was found next day who agreed, for a sum, to take Lalia to Silverstone estate, or what was left of it. The man, old and thin, helped her to load some of her stores and baggage onto the mule. He had brought along a skinny little donkey to ride, and after bidding Mrs Jordan

and her friends farewell, Lalia, in her coolest dress and a
wide, veiled hat, set off with the mulatto following and
leading the mule.

A mile or two out of the town they came to the path of
the hurricane and Lalia was horrified to see the fallen
trees, uprooted bushes, earth ripped from hillsides and
showing ugly red scars, muddy streams where roads had
been, and worst of all, smashed huts, their wooden walls
and roofs scattered over a wide area. A dead mule lay half
under a fallen silk-cotton tree with a cloud of insects
hovering above it.

'Where are all the people?' Lalia asked, lifting her veil
so she could mop her streaming face.

'Dey gone hide in de hills,' he said and refused to meet
her eyes.

Slowly they made their way over the broken land,
seeking a track where there was no danger of being
tripped up by tangled vines and crashed trees, picking
their way around plateaux of oozing ground left by a burst
river bank. As the sun grew hotter, Lalia suffered a
blinding headache and constant irritation from insects.
Her thin clothes clung to her and she realised she would
have been wiser to wear something thicker. Her horse
stumbled and once fell and she suffered a dreadful fear it
had been injured.

When they stopped to eat the food her friends had
provided, she asked, gasping in the relentless heat,

'How much longer?'

The mulatto wiped his mouth after drinking from a
gourd.

' 'Bout tree-four miles mebbe. It go slow when no
road.'

They struggled on. Her skin prickled in the heat until
she could barely endure it. Sweat ran down her face and
trickled down her body. Her horse was showing signs of
fatigue and the mule grew balky and had to be beaten and

sworn at by the guide before it consented to move on again.

Suddenly her guide remarked, with a wave of his hand: 'Cane fields gone to blazes.'

Lalia looked at the fields of smashed cane, beaten down, sometimes uprooted, and a memory uncoiled in her weary mind. '. . . I see a hot sun . . . and not a tree standing . . .' What else had the old gypsy said? But her tired mind could not concentrate. Clinging to her horse, dazed by heat and discomfort and aching bones, she followed the guide through the ruined canefields.

Suddenly his shout made her raise her head and she saw the land ahead rising to a shallow plateau on which stood stone walls, a desolate memorial to a once fine stone and timber planter's home. Smashed wood had been carried to pile against a huddle of wrecked buildings that had been the sugar-mill, boiling house, still and cooling-house.

'House gone,' the guide muttered. 'Nobody go stay here. We go back quick, Ma'am. Here ain't no good.'

'No, wait.' She slipped from her horse and nearly fell as her legs, cramped from the long ride, failed to support her. She grabbed at the saddle, pausing to catch her breath and ease her stiff and aching body. 'Is this Silverstone?'

The man nodded, his eyes rolling nervously from side to side.

'There must be someone here. . .' she started convulsively as a terrified scream tore the air.

'It come—all white and *bad*! *Duppie*!'

She swung around to see the guide turn his donkey and career madly back the way they had come. She called to him, but he paid no heed and continued on his wild race.

A voice called to her and she saw a woman dressed in dirty white with a white cloth over her head coming down from the ruined house, the figure her guide had thought a ghost!

'Who you who come?' As she approached, Lalia saw she was an old negro woman bent with rheumatism. 'De good Lawd send you to help us! Praises be! You got food?'

Lalia stumbled forward to meet her. 'Yes, I have some food. Where is . . . is the owner, Mr Brookford?'

'Mas' Brookford? He sick from fever, Ma'am, sick very bad! He don't eat nothing, only drink water. He talk funny—is the fever, Ma'am.'

'Where is he? I am his wife, take me to him!'

'He lie in little stone store-house, de wind don't mash it down.' She pointed to a small stone building half hidden by debris. 'You come quick, Ma'am. I think it likely he die!'

CHAPTER
TWENTY-ONE

HE lay on a heap of dirty rags, scraps of blankets, curtains and clothing. As her eyes became accustomed to the darkness, Lalia saw his face, flushed and burning, the parched skin strained over the bones and the blank eyes that looked through her and past her and did not see her. She tore off her hat and veil, throwing them in a corner, and knelt down, her heart in her mouth and a terrible dread tearing her.

His cracked lips moved and a dry whisper came from them.

'Get out . . . of the house, Elton, the . . . roof's going! *Look out, man*!' He tried to rise only to fall back panting: 'Water!'

'Bring water,' Lalia commanded without turning her head. 'Is it boiled?'

'Yes, Ma'am, I make a small fire and boil it.' The old woman came in with a calabash filled with water. 'It good to drink.'

'Get me more, I must wash him.' Gently Lalia raised him, her arm around his shoulders, and put the water to his lips and watched him drink thirstily before falling back, his burning eyes closed.

With the old woman's help she washed the burning skin and smoothed out the rags beneath him. At her orders, the woman brought the case of medicines that had been strapped to the mule's back. She worked swiftly, unheeding of the sweat running down her face and the misery of clothing sticking to her body. Romey drank the draught she gave him and lay breathing in quick shallow breaths while she watched him, noting every movement, every difficult breath.

She knelt beside the improvised bed, heedless of her discomfort and the stifling heat of the small room, her whole being concentrated on the man she loved. At intervals she gave him more medicine and bathed his face and body and watched and prayed.

The night came with a suddenness that she was too weary to notice. She felt a steady cooling in the air and thanked God for it. It seemed to her that Romey's breathing was easier and his movements less restless.

'Has he eaten anything?' she asked the old woman.

'De fever don't let him eat, Ma'am, and there ain't much to eat now. Everything smash up in de wind.'

'What happened?' she asked, rising to stretch her aching body. 'Was he hurt?'

'Mas' Brookford got thrown by de wind and knock up 'gainst the cooling-house and lays there two nights before I done find him. Then he get fever bad.'

'What happened to Mr Elton, the overseer? And where are the servants and workers?' Lalia demanded.

'Oh laws, Ma'am, dey run away. Everything blowing down and water come in. No places to sleep and nothing to eat . . . and they frightened of bad sperrits!'

'Are you frightened?' Lalia saw the woman's eyes glance around in fear as she whispered

'I frightened all right—but I don't leave Mas' Brookford; he been mighty good to old Juba. I his cook, Ma'am.'

'God bless you for staying, Juba. Now we must eat. I have stores packed on the mule and horse.'

'I take them off, Ma'am, and tie de animals up so dey doesn't stray. Stores is in that corner.'

Lalia had no appetite, but she forced herself to eat

some of the food she had brought. Juba disappeared and came back holding a slim bottle.

'All ain't smash up in de wine cellar,' her face wrinkled in a wide grin. 'Now you is here, I ain't frightened to go to de house in de dark.'

The wine and food put new life into them, and the cooling air brought relief from some of Lalia's discomforts. She sat beside Romey, brushing away the mosquitoes that hummed around them. Outside, the cicadas trilled and from a nearby pond the twanging notes of the bull frogs kept up a monotonous chorus.

Romey lay on the clean sheet in which she had wrapped some of her stores and was covered with a second one. Sometimes he rolled his head restlessly and broken words and phrases came from his dry lips. Then he would lie still and fear rose in her that life had gone. He took the medicine when she gave it to him and she thought he felt relief when she washed him with cool water.

She had no sensation of time passing, her world had narrowed down to the man burning with fever who must not die. She would not let him die! That he did not love or want her, that perhaps he loved Edwina, did not matter. All that mattered was that Romey, her most dear love, must live!

Juba brought her wine in a coconut shell and whispered: 'I watch now, Ma'am. You go get some fresh air. I wash him and keep off skeeters.'

Lalia hesitated, then obeyed. Outside the little stone hut, she stood breathing in the cool night air in grateful gulps. A great moon had risen, painting the weird landscape in silver slashed with black shadows. A wrecked building placed on higher ground still retained two great iron rollers and must have been the grinding and boiling house. All vestige of the servants' quarters, wooden troughs for the juice from the crushed cane, curing-house and still-house had gone.

A sound from the hut made her re-enter swiftly and she saw Juba crossing herself and muttering rapidly: 'Blessings on de Lawd! He hear our prayers . . . Blessings!'

She sank down beside the sick man and by the light of the one candle Juba had lit, saw the moist sheen on his skin and cried out, 'The fever has broken! Oh—it has broken at last, thank God!'

She burst into tears and felt Juba's arms around her shoulders.

'Ain't nothing to cry over, Ma'am, Mas' Brookford go get well now. You just lay down and sleep 'fore you drop. Juba'll keep watch and give de medicine.'

'But it may be a false drop in temperature,' she bent over him and, touching his forehead, found the skin no longer dry and burning. Romey's breathing had deepened and become regular and he gave a small sigh, as if deeply contented, and slept on.

'Keep him covered now he is sweating,' she ordered, 'and give him this draught if he asks for a drink. Call me the minute you see any change, or if he should awaken.' She knew she was near the end of her endurance and if she did not sleep she would be useless.

There were dry leaves in one corner of the hut, blown in by the wind before the rains came. She sank down on them and was instantly and deeply asleep.

A ray of sunlight coming in through the empty window woke her and she sat up, her hands going to her disordered hair to which dry leaves were clinging.

'How is he, Juba?' She got to her feet and gasped as her aching body rebelled. 'Is the fever better?'

'Fever's gone, Ma'am, angels of God be praised.' Juba's black face was wreathed in smiles as she looked up from Romey's bedside. 'He sleeping like a baby.'

'He must eat something. I have a bottle of jellied chicken soup.'

She stood looking down at the sleeping man, noting the relaxed limbs and moist skin, no longer stretched so taut over the bones, and her heart lifted in a wave of joy so great she felt hot tears sting her eyes.

'Perhaps he could eat a biscuit. Is there any fruit, Juba?'

'Hurricane don't leave no fruit,' Juba grumbled, getting stiffly to her feet. 'It blow away and mash up. Mebbe I can find a pawpaw or mango somewheres. But first I make a fire to warm de soup and boil water.'

Lalia laid her hand gently on Romey's forehead, rejoicing in its coolness. Suddenly his eyelids fluttered, then his eyes opened and looked up into hers.

'Lalia . . .' it was the barest whisper. 'You . . . are here? How . . .'

'Hush, don't try to speak. You must stay still and rest,' she said quickly. 'You have been very ill, but the fever has gone. I am going to give you some soup, but first, take this medicine.'

'Lalia—' he began, but she shook her head and hurried out to get the medicine and measure out a dose. He took it obediently, his eyes never leaving her face. As he lay back, he murmured,

'I don't understand . . . Why are you here?'

'I will explain later, Romey. Now, can you drink a little of this soup?'

He drank some and later, ate a biscuit. Then he sank into sleep again.

There had been a shower in the night and the air was fresh. Lalia got food for herself and Juba and they ate it sitting on a fallen tree trunk outside the hut. Suddenly Lalia remembered something.

'Juba, you did not tell me what happened to the overseer, Mr Elton.'

To her surprise, the old woman rose, mumbling something about washing the dishes in the stream. Lalia caught her skirt.

'I asked you what happened to Mr Elton, did he get away or was he hurt?'

'I don't know nothing 'bout him,' Juba muttered, averting her face. 'Let me go, Ma'am, so's I can wash de dishes.'

But Lalia had seen something in Juba's face that made her tighten her grip on the skirt and say sharply,

'You know something about him. *Was* he hurt? Did he go with the servants?'

'I tells you I don't know nothing!' Juba's cracked voice rose in a shrill scream that brought Lalia to her feet.

'I am your mistress and I *insist* you tell me! *What happened to Mr Elton*?'

The old negro woman's face had become a mask of fear. Her lips trembled and her eyes darted from side to side. She began to pant, her words coming jerkily between frightened gasps.

'I don't know nothing . . . I see nothing! If I speak, *he'll* get me for sure! Big Cutlass soon find I speak and he kill me! I tells you, *I see nothing*!'

'Who is Big Cutlass? *What* did you see?' Lalia gripped the woman's bony shoulders and shook her unmercifully. 'Tell me! I'll—I'll give you no more food until you tell me what you saw, and what you know of Mr Elton. I . . . I'll set the duppies on you.'

'No, no, Ma'am! I don't do you no harm! I look after Mas' Brookford when I finds him! I are a good woman, I don't have nothing to do with Big Cutlass!' Juba sobbed wildly.

'Sit down Juba,' Lalia saw she would get nothing from the woman by threatening her. 'Now, there is nothing to be frightened of while I am here. I shall look after you and no one will kill you. You are safe with Mr Brookford and me. Tell me, who is this Big Cutlass?'

It took half an hour of coaxing, reassuring and scolding and, finally, a drink of wine and—an inspiration on

Lalia's part—the gift of her hat and veil before Juba told her story.

Big Cutlass was a giant negro worker and got his name from the outsize cutlass he used for cutting cane. He was 'bad', Juba said, fighting the other men, stealing and ill-treating their women and slacking at his work. Alvin had turned him away, but he had returned to Silverstone when Romey came, pretending he was a stranger and the other servants and workers were afraid to give him away. Tom Elton had told Romey of the man's reputation and Romey had ordered him off the plantation and the man had gone, swearing revenge.

'When de big wind start,' Juba whispered, 'Big Cutlass return. I see him hide under de banyan tree and I see he got his cutlass with him and I warn Mas' Elton and Mas' Brookford. But Mas' Elton, he don't believe me and he go down to see what happen to de sugar-mill and . . . and Big Cutlass cut him down like he was cutting cane!'

'You mean—he *murdered* him?' Lalia felt a chill creep over her.

Juba looked away. 'Mas' Elton dead all right.'

'What did the man do with the—the body?'

'He throw it in de river—and go away *laughing*!' Juba crossed herself with a shaking hand.

For a moment Lalia felt something of the old woman's horror. Then she rose and said, keeping her voice light with an effort, 'You did right to tell me, Juba, and I shall see no harm comes to you. Big Cutlass was probably killed in the hurricane. Now please wash some of the clothes I wore yesterday while I give my husband some more soup.'

For the rest of the day Romey was too weak to do more than smile at her and take what food and medicine she offered and sleep. Lalia was astonished and heartened at how swiftly he seemed to be recovering from the fever. While he slept, she went with Juba up to the ruined house

that had been Alvin's and to which he had taken Rosa.
The wooden part had been swept away, but the stone
foundation walls remained and in the cellars beneath
them Lalia found more wine and a small store of flour,
sugar and dried pulses and a few cooking utensils.
Shattered glass, splintered furniture, remnants of curtains, bedding and carpets, told of the storm's fury. But
she had no time to think of it now; to restore Romey
back to health and get him to a town was all that
mattered.

Juba had concocted a cooking-pit out of earth and two
bricks and on this she cooked such food as they had and
boiled water for drinking. She had taken charge of the two
animals and kept them fed and watered.

On the third day Romey sat up and put aside the gruel
she offered him.

'Lalia, tell me how you came to be here, and when, and
why. I don't understand. I've been wondering if I've been
seeing fever-visions.'

'I heard about the earthquake and hurricane,' she said,
keeping her eyes on the dish she held, 'and I got a passage
out on the *Sea Queen*. A guide brought me here where I
found you ill with fever and only Juba in charge.'

'You came seeking me?' His eyes, clear and intent,
searched her face. '*Why*, Lalia?'

She hesitated, then because there must no longer be
any misunderstanding between them, she raised her eyes
to his and said, 'I had to come. I was afraid you might be
hurt. I *had* to come.'

There was a silence in which she could hear Juba's
tuneless crooning outside the hut.

'Because you considered it to be your duty as my wife?'
he put a hand on her arm.

'No. Because I discovered . . . I love you, Romey.'

His grip on her arm was surprisingly strong for a sick
man.

'You mean that? Don't lie to me, Lalia.'

She shook her head. 'I haven't lied this time, but I *did* lie about Malcolm. I never loved him, *never*. But I wanted to hurt you and make you angry . . . because of Edwina.'

'Edwina? What in heaven's name has she to do with anything?'

'I thought you still loved her.'

His eyes widened, then he drew her nearer. 'Oh, my stupid darling! How could I love her when I was so deeply, achingly in love with my wife, a wife who wanted only to be my friend.'

It was true! She heard it in his voice and saw it in his face!

'You did not love me when you asked me to marry you.'

'No. But there was something about you . . . I used to dream of you when I was a boy. I thought I had done with love, but I wanted you for my wife. And afterwards,' he held her hand against his cheek and then turned his head and kissed it gently, 'I fell in love with you. I went through hell, loving you and wanting you, trying to keep away from you because love was not part of your bargain. When you flirted with Voizard . . . but you weren't serious about that, I knew. But Malcolm was different, he was in love with you—and you said you loved him! I couldn't stand it any more, so I went away.'

'I did not know I loved you until you left me,' she said softly. 'I was so terribly jealous of Edwina.'

'It was crazy to think I could ever have anything but pity, and kindness, for her. Her marriage was most unhappy.'

'I think she still loves you; and she resented me.'

'Because you were happy and she has never been happy, that is why I felt sorry for her.'

'I am sorry too, now I know,' she said soberly. 'Romey, will you come back to England—and me?'

He smiled into her eyes. 'Try and stop me, you wicked witch,' and kissed her with a longing that told her all she wished to know.

Romey insisted that in a few days he would be able to ride back to St Anna. Lalia was dubious, but secretly she longed to leave the wrecked estate with its unhappy memories of Alvin and Rosa, and Juba's story of Elton's murder still haunted her and brought her bad dreams. When Romey asked about his overseer, she lied and said she knew nothing. It would be time enough when he was fully recovered for him to know the ugly truth.

He was weak at first when he moved about, but his strength returned surprisingly quickly. He uncovered another store of food that had survived the storm and the three of them gathered remains of curtains and carpets for makeshift beds. The weather had stayed reasonably cool and there were showers to keep the air fresh.

One afternoon Romey was sleeping in the hut while Lalia stirred a potful of porridge made from dried peas over the fire outside. Suddenly a primitive instinct warned her and she swung around and a scream of fear died in her throat.

He stood looking at her, his heavy shoulders slightly bent and his head thrust forward. Something flashed in the sunlight and she saw the great curved knife in his hand as he swung it gently to and fro.

'Danger . . .' something whispered inside her head, 'be careful of the big knife . . .'

Frozen with fear, she managed to gasp: 'Who—who are you? What do you want?'

He turned his head, peering in the doorway of the hut where Romey lay sleeping, and a grin split the sweating blackness of his face.

'*He* know who I am! He send me away like I was dirt!' He spoke in a curiously soft, sibilent voice that struck terror into her heart. 'I don't 'low no man to treat me like I was dirt! No man going to tell Big Cutlass he no good. You his woman?'

'I—I am his wife. You must go away, at once!' As he came near she caught the smell of the rank local rum. 'Go away!' She kept her voice low, terrified Romey would waken.

'One man here treat me ugly—and he ain't here no more now. Git outa my way, woman. No man treat me like dirt and stay 'live!'

He took a step towards the hut. Without thinking, without planning, moving in a lightning flash, she seized the pot of boiling porridge and hurled it straight in his face!

He screamed, his hands going to his face, the knife falling from his grasp. In a second she had it in her hands and with all her strength she struck . . . and struck . . . and struck again!

Light stabbed her eyes, the sun spun in an arc around her and she shrank back, gasping. Then the mists before her eyes cleared and she saw him staggering drunkenly down the hill, screaming, his hands clawing at his face.

She let the cutlass drop and stood staring stupidly at the blood on it before she sank down into blackness.

CHAPTER
TWENTY-TWO

'LALIA.' Romey's voice came through the blackness, dissolving it into a grey mist that slowly dispersed as she opened her eyes to see his face bending over her. 'Lalia, my dearest, are you hurt?'

'She fainted,' said a woman's voice she recognised. 'She'll be all right, Mr Brookford. Give her some of this brandy.'

The raw spirit made her choke, but she felt her mind clear as she caught at Romey's arm.

'He was going to kill you—as he killed Mr Elton! Juba told me . . . He wanted to *kill* you!'

'It was Big Cutlass, wasn't it, Mrs Brookford?' a man's voice asked and she looked up to see a sun-tanned man standing beside Mrs Jordan.

'Yes,' Lalia whispered and felt Romey's arm tighter around her. 'Where is he? He may come back! He wants to kill Romey!'

'Don't worry, Mrs Brookford,' the man said, 'we've got him. We found him washing his wounds in the river, he seemed half-blinded. He's wanted for two other murders.'

'I threw the pot of porridge in his face,' Lalia said, sitting up and brushing back the tendrils of fair hair from her face, 'then I got his knife and . . .' she turned and buried her face in Romey's shoulder.

His hand caressed her tangled hair gently. 'My brave girl. You saved my life. I wouldn't have had a chance if he had got into the hut.'

Two men now came up and one said: 'Nothing much left of your house I'm afraid, Brookford, and the cane's gone. Some of your workers have returned and I'm setting them to start clearing up. But there is little you can do here and I advise you to take your wife to St Anna. You're still pretty weak, you know. I'll stay and see to the work here until you send someone.'

'I'll be grateful if you can do that, many thanks.' He helped Lalia to her feet. 'I think we'll start back right away if my wife feels strong enough.'

'Oh yes, please,' Lalia said quickly 'I—I don't want to stay here. And Romey should see a doctor. Thank you so much for coming—but why did you not come before?'

'We heard your husband had drowned, Mrs Brook-ford, someone had seen his body in the river. It was only a few days ago that it was recovered and proved to be that of poor Elton. When you did not return, we set out.'

'And I insisted on coming too,' Mrs Jordan said. 'I've been terribly worried about you, child, but the roads were impassable and I'm no horsewoman. Thank God they have cleared some of the roads now. We have managed to bring a cart so your husband need not ride.'

'But we cannot leave Juba,' Lalia pleaded, looking at Romey, '*she* saved your life by caring for you.'

'I'll look after her,' one of the men promised. 'We've brought stores and the workers will soon manage some sort of shelter until the huts can be rebuilt. She'll be all right, Mrs Brookford.'

'I shall see she is all right for the rest of her life,' Romey promised. 'We'll leave our medical supplies, you may need them, and I will send someone from St Anna to relieve you. As yet, I haven't made plans for the future.'

Lalia leaned against his arm, her eyes thoughtful. Would Romey agree to *her* plan, that they take passage back to England, to Dorset and Hildon Manor, their home? That Silverstone with its tragic memories be sold?

The island would recover in time, its lush vegetation springing into new life and covering the ravages of the past. Homes would be rebuilt, canes replanted, rivers return to their natural courses and life in this sun-filled island blaze into renewed colour, richness and promise. But she prayed silently that she and Romey would never return.

She looked up to see his eyes upon her and knew that he guessed her thoughts. He said, 'We'll go home, Lalia.'

'He knows me so well,' she thought, 'and I know him at last. Because we love each other.'

The journey was slow, but not too uncomfortable. In the town, Mrs Jordan took charge and Lalia and Romey was installed in her friends' house while enquiries for a homebound ship were made. The planter whose estate bordered Silverstone agreed to look after it while reconstruction work went on and, Romey told Lalia, was interested in eventually buying the estate.

'So you need never return,' she exclaimed. 'Oh Romey, how wonderful to be going home.'

'To spend the rest of your life loving me, looking after me like a devoted wife, obeying my every wish—'

'Certainly not!' She looked at him, her eyes sparkling. 'Well . . . not *every* wish. We did make a bargain.'

He pulled her into his arms, smiling down into her eyes. 'I have made a new one; we are both free—to love each other to the end of our lives.'

'But—' she got no further. He kissed her, gently at first, then with passion and longing that made her cling to him, knowing that this was what her heart had always hungered for: Romey, her husband and her lover.

The ship heeled gently into the wind, rising and dipping as if curtseying a farewell to the green and gold island it was leaving. Lalia, standing at the rails beside Romey, watched the widening expanse of water separate her from the land that had so nearly taken her husband from her.

She slid her arm through his. 'Romey, did you find out anything more about Alvin and Rosa?'

He shook his head. His skin had taken on a healthy tan and he had regained some of the weight the fever had taken from him.

'Alvin drank himself to death, poor fellow, and had no strength to fight when the fever took him. No one spoke of Rosa to me. Theirs is a tragic story, my dearest, let us forget it.'

'Willingly,' she agreed, and had a moment of deep pity and sadness for the man she had once thought to marry and the woman who had thrown away everything for her lover, only to be rejected.

Then she felt Romey's arms around her holding her closely and her happiness, like a golden cloak of joy and fulfilment, wrapped around her, making her indeed a Gold Bride, golden in Romey's love and the rich promise of the future.

'We are going home,' she murmured, and knew the words held all she wished for in life.

'Going home,' he said, 'together, my most dear wife of my heart.'

Masquerade
Historical Romances

Intrigue
excitement
romance

Don't miss
March's
other enthralling Historical Romance title

PRINCE OF DECEPTION
by Valentina Luellen

Emma Fraser willingly accompanies her spoilt cousin Anne to Russia in 1761, where she is to marry Prince Nikolai Adashev, for it can hardly be worse than her present life as unpaid drudge.

On their arrival in St Petersburg she is horrified to find that the man she took to be a fellow servant is Prince Michael, head of the House of Adashev. It is Michael who has arranged Anne's marriage, and he has plans for Emma too . . . But how can she trust him when he has already deceived her once? Especially when he seems to be so closely involved with the Czarina Catherine.

As Catherine's struggle for control of the country intensifies Emma is caught up in the fierce battle – and the man she most mistrusts is the one man she finds irresistible.

You can obtain this title today from your local paperback retailer

Masquerade
Historical Romances

Intrigue excitement romance

THE KING'S FAVOURITE
by Caroline Martin

When Sir Gavin Hamilton is spurned by the lovely Honoria Somervell he vows to bring about her downfall. To his surprise he is unable to carry out his threats. Can it be that he needs love more than all the things he has fought for – power, wealth and the king's favour?

PIONEER GIRL
by Margaret Pemberton

To the small band of pioneers struggling towards the Rocky Mountains in the bitter winter of 1846 the chance meeting with Major Dart Richards is a fateful encounter. And to the orphaned Polly Kirkham it is especially disturbing. But the Major has vowed never again to become involved with a woman, so why does he find himself accompanying them across the icy wastes in pursuit of an ideal?

Look out for these titles in your local paperback shop from 9th April 1982